OUT of HIDING

Catherine Farnes

JOURNEY BOOKS
Greenville, South Carolina

YA
FAR

Library of Congress CIP data:
Farnes, Catherine, 1964-
   Out of hiding / Catherine Farnes.
      p. cm.
   Summary: While on a missionary trip to Mexico, Ashton encounters fear, doubt, and danger, but the most difficult to deal with is the painful memory of her brother's death.
   ISBN 1-57924-329-0
    [1. Missionaries—Fiction. 2. Christian life—Fiction. 3. Death—Fiction. 4. Mexico—Fiction.] I. Title.

PZ7.F238365 Ou 2000
[Fic]—dc21   99-088171

Out of Hiding

Editor: Gloria Repp
Project Editor: Debbie L. Parker
Designed by Duane A. Nichols
Cover by Mary Ann Lumm

© 2000 Bob Jones University Press
Greenville, South Carolina 29614

ISBN 1-57924-329-0

15   14   13   12   11   10 9 8 7 6 5 4 3 2 1

For Chris and Rocio,
Steven, Christopher, and Jeanelle

Books by Catherine Farnes

The Rivers of Judah

Snow

Out of Hiding

Contents

Chapter One 1

Chapter Two 7

Chapter Three 11

Chapter Four 19

Chapter Five 29

Chapter Six 39

Chapter Seven 53

Chapter Eight 61

Chapter Nine 71

Chapter Ten 79

Chapter Eleven 93

Chapter Twelve 103

Chapter Thirteen 109

Chapter Fourteen 115

Chapter Fifteen 123

Chapter Sixteen 131

Chapter Seventeen 139

Chapter Eighteen 147

Chapter Nineteen 157

Chapter Twenty 165

Chapter Twenty-One 171

Can any hide himself in secret places
that I shall not see him? saith the Lord.
Do not I fill heaven and earth? saith the Lord.
                                            —Jeremiah 23:24

Chapter 1

It wasn't until I actually saw Mr. Cirone and his wife that it occurred to me to be nervous. I recognized them immediately because their picture was at the bottom of the letter they'd sent to let me know that my place on the summer mission team had been confirmed.

This was the real thing.

Seven months ago, our youth pastor had handed out copies of a letter he'd received from a mission board. Each year it sent a team of ten kids to the foreign field to offer assistance to a missionary. Our youth pastor thought we'd find the letter particularly interesting because this year the missionary the team would be visiting had been sent out by our church. Two of us, Chad Reese and I, had sent in applications. Both of us had been accepted.

And now, after months of fundraising, planning, praying, and anticipating, we were finally here.

I smiled and approached the Cirones.

Chad moved slightly ahead of me and held out his hand. "I'm Chad Reese," he said to Mr. Cirone. "And this is Ashton Cook."

Mr. Cirone greeted us warmly. "Good flight?"

I nodded. Our flights from Anchorage to El Paso had been completely uneventful. As far as I was concerned, *uneventful* and *good* were synonymous when it came to flying.

Mr. and Mrs. Cirone quickly introduced us to Mr. Marsh, our third adult chaperone, and to the six kids on the team who had already arrived. Four boys. Two girls. I looked at each one, repeating their names to myself silently, three times. I didn't want to spend any of our time—four days here in Texas and then three weeks in Mexico—being confused about who was who. Todd. Matt. Alec. Shane. Hope. Callie.

"You're the next to last to come in," Mr. Marsh said, "so we'll pick up your bags and hurry over to our last gate."

"Why couldn't you people get morning flights?" one of the girls muttered in my direction as she pushed past me.

I gave the girl—Callie—a curious frown. As if I'd had anything to do with the scheduling of flights out of Alaska!

It seemed to me, as our group walked through the airport, that uneasiness was the prevalent emotion among us teenagers. It wasn't hard to figure out why. This would likely be the farthest from home most of us had traveled . . . if not in the number of miles, certainly in respect to cultural differences.

And for me, this would be my first time in a situation in which everyone around me except Chad would be a stranger. Other than my brother's death and our pastor's resignation because so many people thought the drowning accident had been his son's fault, life had been routine and predictable. People didn't come and go much. And when anyone new had come into the church or its Christian school where I attended, I was always the hostess doing the welcoming. Showing him or her around my favorite places.

Now I was about to step onto the soil of a strange country with eight teenagers I'd never met and be under the care of three adults who knew nothing about me other than what I'd written on my missions application.

Scary.

Well . . . I did know Dane Meyer. He was the missionary we'd be helping. We were all going to build the first Christian church in the remote village where he lived. He had been my fifth- and sixth-grade Sunday school teacher. He'd been working in Mexico for five years, so I was excited to see him again. And curious to see if he'd remember me.

As we walked toward the baggage claim area and then out onto the main concourse, a couple of the boys talked quietly and with a lot of pauses about a sports team, and Callie was jabbering to nobody in particular about how she'd always hated airports.

But Hope, after a few minutes, stepped up to walk beside me. "Did I hear Mr. Cirone right? You're from Alaska?"

I looked at Hope, an attractive but not gorgeous reddish-blond who looked like the type to squeal whenever she saw a spider. I smiled. "Yeah."

"I've always wanted to go there," she said.

Her easy chatter about all the things she'd ever wanted to do in Alaska and then about her home in New York and the kind of clothes she'd brought for the trip—all made even more enjoyable by her healthy Long Island accent—reassured me. We wouldn't be a group of strangers for very long.

We arrived at the gate where we'd pick up the last two team members and got busy about loading our bags onto a cart Mr. Cirone had found. Everyone helped him arrange the bags so that none of them would fall off on our way out to the parking lot. Everyone but Callie. She stood apart from the group, leaning against a pole with her arms folded across her stomach, watching someone in the crowd.

After handing her bag and mine to Mr. Cirone, Hope sat down in a nearby chair. "Why does there always have to be one obnoxious person in every group?"

I sat beside her and shrugged.

"There's one in math class, in youth group, in choir." She shook her head. "Everywhere you get a group of kids together, there's always someone being obnoxious."

I smiled, but did not reply. In my life, the "obnoxious person" in every group had been my brother Tommy. He wasn't obnoxious in the same ways that Callie had been thus far, but he had been the rule-challenger, the joker, the one who had to test the limits. I knew that he had acted that way in response to the pressure he felt to be a certain way because he was the assistant pastor's son. The pressure never came from my father, or even from our pastor or youth leader. My brother had built it up inside himself . . . partially, I'd always thought, because his best friend, our pastor's oldest son, was practically perfect. At least that was the going consensus among our congregation. Perfectly behaved, neatly dressed, excellent grades, always pointing out that such and such was the right thing to do, never a sour look from anyone. The fact that my brother had maintained a close friendship with such a "what a nice young man" boy had always amazed me.

I tried to chase away the images of my brother by looking at Callie. Tall. Dark hair. Green eyes. Fit.

"What are you looking at?" she asked when she noticed that I'd been staring at her. She stepped away from the pole. "If you're going to gawk at anyone . . ." She paused to point at Hope. "It should be her." She laughed. "A little chunky, aren't you, to be thinking about hiking through the jungle?"

I turned away before I could spit out an insult of my own. I didn't know what Callie's problem was, and I didn't care. But she didn't have to be such a jerk to a stranger. Besides, Hope wasn't chunky! She wasn't Miss Let's See How Thin We Can Get and Still Not See Our Skeletal Structure Right Under Our Skin . . . but neither was I. For that matter, neither was Callie! And who wanted to be?

I could tell by the way Hope pretended to be distracted by someone walking past that the comment had hurt her. But she said nothing.

After a long stare at a nearby wall, Callie looked uncomfortably at Hope. "I'm sorry," she said. "I . . . oh, never mind."

Then the announcement came that the plane we were waiting for had landed. Passengers would be entering the gate area in just a few moments. The familiar excitement I'd felt about this trip for months tightened my stomach and kept me from being able to sit still.

In a matter of moments we'd be meeting our final two team members and heading to Mr. Cirone's church for a special dinner and Get-Acquainted meeting—the real beginning of our mission trip.

I had no idea, really, what to expect from the three weeks ahead of me, but I was definitely eager to experience them. And I was going to be on my own enough—away from all the religious structure that had always been provided for me—to hopefully find out what I was really made of. What I did and didn't believe for myself. What kind of faith I had . . .

Or didn't have.

When I heard Mr. Cirone welcoming someone to Texas, I shouldered my carryon bag and turned toward his voice to be introduced. I stepped back in disbelief before I realized I was doing it and gripped the back of the nearest chair.

Judah Ewen.

Our former pastor's son.

He looked different . . . older, taller, stronger . . . but it was definitely him.

And a girl. Rebekah something. I heard Mr. Cirone say her name. I smiled and probably said hello when I shook her hand . . . but my mind was trapped in that one instant when I first saw Judah.

And then, before I could think about how I should respond to him, he was standing in front of me.

"Ash," he said quietly.

I'd forgotten that he'd called me that.

I smiled and shook his hand . . . as if I was meeting him for the first time. I didn't know what else to do. Then I watched as Chad did the same. Neither boy looked directly at the other.

Mr. Cirone directed us to a less-crowded corner of the gate area. "This is it," he said. "This is the team. Are we ready?"

Ready?

Not at all. Not anymore.

Chapter 2

When Hope, sitting beside me at the table, stood to take her turn at introducing herself, I realized I was absently pushing my uneaten peas back and forth across my plate with my fork. I wondered how long I'd been doing that and if anyone had noticed.

"My name is Hope Ferrin," she said. "I'm eighteen. My father pastors on Long Island. I'm going to be a sophomore in college this fall, majoring in Political Science." She smiled. "I came on this mission trip because I'm interested in other cultures, especially those that are a lot different from ours." She directed her next comment to Mr. Cirone. "I'm curious about how we'll communicate the gospel when there are so many barriers to overcome."

"You'll be amazed," Mr. Cirone promised her. Then he motioned for me to stand and take my turn. We had just finished the meal at his church and were almost done with our Get-Acquainted session.

I stood. "I'm Ashton Cook. I'm from Alaska. My dad's an assistant pastor. I just finished my junior year of high school." I looked to the head of the table at Mr. Cirone. "I came on this trip because I wanted to do something for God on my own." I decided not to elaborate further. These were total strangers, after all. And Judah Ewen. "Dane Meyer used to be my Sunday school teacher, so I'm looking forward to seeing him again."

Mr. Cirone nodded at Rebekah. "Your turn."

"My name's Rebekah." Realizing that she'd forgotten to stand, she pushed her chair back from the table and got to her feet. "I'm seventeen, I just graduated, and I'm not really sure what I'll end up doing." She paused. "I came on this trip because, when I prayed about it, I knew God wanted me to."

Mr. Cirone nodded. "Okay, Callie. Your turn."

She stood, shoved her hands into her pockets, and looked down at her plate as she spoke. "I'm Callie. I'm seventeen. I came on this trip because my mother wanted it for me. She thought it would be good for me."

The slight irritability in her tone didn't cover up the tenderness that had suddenly come up in her eyes the way she was probably hoping it would. Instead, it spotlighted it so that I as well as the others—judging by the stilled expressions of everyone at the table—got a first glimpse of Callie the Human Being.

I hoped it wouldn't be our last.

"This trip can be good for you," Mrs. Cirone said quietly. Knowingly.

"I'm sorry I didn't help you guys at the airport," Callie said. "With all the bags and stuff. I was . . . watching someone who . . . looked like someone."

Mr. Cirone nodded and pointed at Chad. "Your turn."

"I'm Chad," he said as he stood up. "I'm eighteen. I decided to come on this trip to see if missionary work might be something I'd like to do with my life, you know, for God."

Chad's remarks lacked his usual enthusiasm when speaking about missions. No doubt because of Judah Ewen's presence at the table.

After the remaining boys—including Judah—had taken their turns, Mr. Cirone pushed his chair slightly back from the table and looked slowly around at each one of us. "You all have your reasons for coming on this trip," he said. "Building the church is the physical thing we're going to Mexico to do. But that's far from all that this is about. Physically, those people could build their own church. And that's exactly what they would do if we weren't going." He smiled. "Number one, we're going to be witnesses. To give the gospel to those who haven't already heard it from Dane. To be an encouragement to those who have . . . and to Dane."

Mrs. Cirone smiled. "Even something as simple as having the opportunity to speak his own language for a couple of weeks can be amazingly encouraging for someone who has been in a foreign place for as long as Dane has," she said. "And to have people from back home come to share his work. His life, really."

Mr. Cirone nodded. "And, on top of all that," he said, "I know that God has things in store for you there too. He always does. Maybe a couple of you, like Chad, are thinking about doing missionary work in the future. This'll definitely give you a taste." He chuckled a little. "Just working together in the heat down there can be a growth experience all on its own."

I had no doubt that was true.

"So . . . " Mr. Cirone rubbed his hands together. "Any questions or concerns?"

There were many. And one issue at a time—everything from whether or not there would be electricity in the village to how to avoid an attack by killer insects to "Is it really true that we shouldn't eat the lettuce?"—Mr. Cirone, his wife, and Mr. Marsh answered them.

"We're going to spend four days here in Texas before driving down to Mexico," Mr. Marsh reminded us after one too many less-than-serious questions about the reptilian perils of the jungle. "That's plenty of time to go over most of the things about this trip that any group of teens would struggle with. Don't worry. We're all going to survive this thing. Nobody's going to be devoured by a giant lizard."

"But," Mrs. Cirone said, "we're going to teach you some basic first aid so you'll know what to do in case someone does get hurt." She sat straighter in her chair and reached up to readjust the wooden clip holding her bangs back away from her face. Her thick blonde hair was in that halfway stage between short and long and was no doubt driving her crazy.

Mr. Cirone cleared his throat. "We're going to learn four skits, which we'll perform in various villages on our way down to where Dane is located. I'll drill you in some basic Spanish. And, of course, I'll tell you about the people Dane ministers to—and exactly how we're going to help them build their church." He stood. "Our first order of business is to let you know who your team partner is going to be. Each of you will have one. This is a safety measure, so nobody has to go anywhere alone. You'll help each other. You'll be assigned to work teams together. And hopefully, you'll get a good start on a lifelong friendship." He took the list from his wife and said, "We chose the partners alphabetically. So, ladies, it'll be Rebekah and Ashton, and Hope and Callie. Guys . . ."

I forced myself to smile at Rebekah. She'd arrived with Judah. Did she know about my brother's death? About how we'd responded? About me? Had she paid attention to my name?

She smiled back.

"Your host families are waiting outside," Mr. Cirone said. "They'll be bringing you to the church at 7:00 A.M., so don't stay up too late chatting with your partner. Hope, would you pray, please?"

We bowed our heads.

"Lord, please help us to bring You glory on this trip. Help us to work together. Help us to stay safe. Thank You for bringing each of us here. We know You have Your reasons. Amen."

I grabbed my bag and followed Rebekah outside. When we climbed into the van with our host family, she busied herself in conversation with them while I stared out the window and tried to make sense of the completely unexpected events of the past two hours.

Chapter 3

The next four days, training days, went well and quickly. Most of the time, everyone seemed eager enough to work, earning comments of praise from Mr. Cirone or his wife, or from Mr. Marsh. And when the work for each day was finished, the adults graciously indulged our desire to clown around a little. Mrs. Cirone took us girls bowling one afternoon, and then to eat ice cream, and then to try on hats in a department store. At first, we were cautious about which hats we'd allow her to prop on our heads, but by the time we'd been there half an hour, we were all laughing. Our choices became more and more exotic, as did our attempts to model them.

Each of us left with a hat. We'd appreciate them during our long hours in the sun, Mrs. Cirone assured us. Mine was teal, made of soft straw with a rolled brim. Something I knew I'd never have thought of buying in Alaska, where the bin on the floor in my closet contained nothing but winter hats and baseball caps.

The person on the team who seemed to have the most trouble relaxing during these "off" times was Mr. Marsh. Being twenty-six, he was younger than Mr. Cirone and intensely aware of his responsibility as a team leader. But none of us doubted his competence.

His blue eyes were always watchful, always alert. Nothing was going to get by him. He was a worker too. Tall. Strong. Precise. If anything during this trip came down to getting done by sheer strength and determination, Mr. Marsh would be the first one there doing it. Every once in a while, he'd tell a joke or a quick comeback to something one of us had said, and we'd all laugh . . . amazed that something so funny could find its way out of such a quiet and guarded man.

Chad was quiet too. Sulky. But so far, at least, he'd had the sense to keep away from Judah and to let Judah keep away from him.

The exciting certainty that we'd be leaving for real in the morning turned all of us a little quiet during our final day of training. So we spent the last two hours of it in group prayer. Safety. Health. Real opportunities to minister the gospel. We prayed for all of it. Everything we could think of.

Then we left with our host families for our last American meals, our last night's sleep on comfortable beds, and our last hot showers. In the morning, we'd climb into the vans and head into a different world.

But for tonight . . . Rebekah and I wanted pizza.

Our host mother ordered it for us, and while we waited for it to arrive, I decided to call my parents. I hadn't talked to them since leaving Alaska.

Rebekah stood as I picked up the phone. "I'll wait in the other room."

"Thanks."

Rebekah had tried several times during the past four days to initiate a conversation with me that would venture beyond what we'd like for dinner or which of the two beds in our host family's guest room I'd prefer, but I was purposely keeping my distance until I could figure out what she knew about me—if anything. She hadn't said anything to me about my brother's death . . . but she never mentioned Judah either, which seemed suspicious considering their obvious friendship.

I'd considered talking to Mrs. Cirone about switching partners . . . how could I build a friendship and function as a "trail buddy" with someone who might know everything about me already—from the Ewens' perspective?

But I hadn't yet figured out what I'd say, exactly, to explain my discomfort with Rebekah. I'd have to dredge up old details, which would dredge up old pain, which would undoubtedly affect the team's unity.

No. I was a big girl. I'd just have to work it out for myself.

My father answered on the second ring, and we spoke for several minutes. I didn't mention Judah. After saying a quicker *hello* and *see you in three weeks* to Mom, I hung up and joined Rebekah in the den.

We sat side by side for several minutes without speaking. I could hear the steady hum of the ceiling fan above our heads. Finally, without looking over at me, Rebekah asked, "Did you tell your parents that Judah is here?"

So she does know.

"No," I said.

More silence.

Now what? I wondered.

Quietly, Rebekah said, "I thought maybe we should get things out in the open before we actually leave for Mexico . . . you know, if you want to switch partners, or anything."

"What has Judah told you?" I asked, more coldly than I'd intended. "Sorry. I didn't mean to sound like that. I just . . . I need to know what you know." I forced myself to look at her—eye to eye. "And what you think about it."

She nodded. "Okay. I know that your brother drowned. I know that a lot of the people in your church blamed Judah. I know that Pastor Ewen lost his church over it." She paused but never looked away from me. "I know it must have been horrible for all of you."

"It was," I agreed. "But it was two years ago. People move on."

"Two years isn't so long," she pointed out.

"Okay, yeah, you're right," I said. "But the point is, I'm not willing to give up on this trip, and I doubt Judah's ready to do that either. So we're here, and we might as well make the best of it."

I smiled. A little. "I'll just avoid him."

Rebekah nodded. "But you can't avoid me. Not if we're partners."

"Are you planning to make me want to avoid you?"

Now it was her turn to smile. "No, Ashton. What's between you and Judah is between you and Judah. And God, of course. I don't think it's my place to get in the middle."

"I can live with that, then." I leaned back and stared up at the ceiling fan.

Our pizza arrived, we ate it, and afterward went to our room to pack for Mexico.

Mr. Cirone had given each team member a backpack and a list of essentials. Everything we brought to Mexico had to fit in the pack. No exceptions. We'd be doing a lot of walking during our trip because hiking was the only way to get into some of the deep jungle villages we'd be visiting.

With the packs, we'd been given sleeping bags, our own bottles of sunscreen, insect repellent, water purification tablets, various stomach remedies, antibacterial soap, matches, a pocketknife, and a small first-aid kit. We each had our own plate, cup, and silverware—the blue-white speckled stuff. Sunglasses. Our hats. A second pair of boots, which we'd tie to our pack frames.

Other than that, we could pack whatever clothes we thought we'd need that would fit in the pack. Mr. Cirone had also handed out zippered pouches which tied around our waists beneath our clothes for our money, identification papers, and all our legal documents.

"Did you bring long pants?" Rebekah asked me.

"Jeans, mostly. I don't want my legs getting all scratched up."

She lifted a sweatshirt out of her pack, held it for an undecided moment above the pile of clothes she couldn't fit in, then packed it again. "These packs fill up fast, don't they?"

I nodded. "We'll be glad, when we're hiking, that we didn't have room for those four extra sweatshirts."

She pulled the sweatshirt back out of the pack. This time, it stayed out. "Do you think we'll have many chances to wash our clothes?"

"I hope so!"

Rebekah watched me toss a couple of hair accessories into the top pouch of my pack. "You have pretty hair, Ashton."

"Thanks. So do you." I decided to change the subject. "Are you nervous? About actually going to Mexico?"

"A little," she said. "I just hope we don't all get sick."

"I'm sure Mr. Cirone is bringing stuff for that," I said.

She nodded, but her expression remained unconvinced. "Pastor Ewen told us about this time when a youth group came to visit him while he was doing missionary work in South America, and all of them—all twenty of them—got sick."

I remembered Pastor Ewen speaking frequently about his work in missions. His excitement. His conviction.

"Could you imagine," Rebekah went on, "twenty kids, all sick, in a house with only one bathroom?"

"I don't want to imagine."

"He said the toilet was flushing all night long."

"Nasty," I said, laughing now. "He told you this from the pulpit?"

"No!"

"Good," I said. "I know how he likes to keep his sermons real, but that would be a bit much."

We laughed.

"No," she said. "He told my family one night while we were having dinner at their house."

"Oh, and dinner's a much better place to talk about stuff like that." I grinned. Hadn't he done the same thing to my family more than once? "How appetizing."

"No doubt," she said. "But then he told us that those same twenty kids got to lead almost an entire village to Christ."

"Wow."

"Then," she said, "he told us about this hotel he stayed in where you could help yourself to some fresh-brewed coffee. Well, he took the last cup, so he thought he'd be Christlike and start another pot going . . . "

I remembered this story and held up my hand to stop her, but she didn't notice.

"Except, when he pulls out the filter drawer to take out the grounds, they're *moving!*"

"*Yuck!*" I squealed. "Yuck."

"Then—"

"Please," I begged, "I know his stories, and I don't want to hear any more." I smiled. "Not the night before heading down there."

So we went quiet again.

As much as I hated to acknowledge it, and though I'd never admit it aloud, I missed Pastor Ewen's preaching. I missed him. And his wife. Our two families had been close . . . but then there'd been Judah's camping trip with my brother. And . . . Tommy's death.

When I'd finished packing, I tied my hiking boots to my pack and lugged it into the bathroom. I hefted it onto my back and stood on the scale. 145 pounds. Then I lowered the pack to the floor. Without it, I weighed 118. Knowing from past experience that I could easily carry a 27-pound pack, I brought it downstairs and set it by the front door. I'd already chosen my clothes for the morning and had placed them, and the pouch I'd wear underneath them, on top of my shoes on the floor at the foot of my bed.

Rebekah and I chatted only briefly before turning off the light and getting to bed for the night. I rolled onto my side and closed my eyes, even though I knew I wouldn't be able to sleep.

In less than twelve hours, I'd be in Mexico!

Chapter 4

The first day, spent on a paved road heading south and then west to Poza Rica, a city of about half a million people, might not have seemed like much of an adventure, but the second day promised to make up for it.

We spent the night in the auditorium of a church that had been started by one of Dane Meyer's converts. The man and his congregation had welcomed us as if we were long-lost family. Several women had prepared meals in their homes and had brought them to the church for us. Soft white corn tortillas made by hand, thick and fresh—wrapped in a cloth. Spanish rice. And *mole*—a combination of unsweetened chocolate, chicken broth, and a mixture of nuts and chilies all ground into a thick brown gravy—poured over boiled chicken. The *mole* had been a unique eating experience—one I'd probably try to avoid in the future. The rest of the meal, however, could not have been more delicious. In addition to the genuine hospitality of the women, we'd enjoyed a brief welcome from the pastor, translated by Mr. Cirone, and then a song performed for us by the church's children:

> *Bienvenidos sean, hermanos,*
> *En el nombre bendito de Dios.*
> *Hoy reunidos nos gozamos*
> *Al saber que nos une su amor . . .*

Even though I'd had no idea what the words to the song meant, the energetic and enthusiastic smiles of the children as they sang and clapped made their intention obvious. They wanted to welcome us warmly.

And they had.

Then, we had slept . . . on top of our sleeping bags on the wooden benches that occupied the front half of the building. One of the boys talked about putting his sleeping bag on the floor and sleeping there, but Mr. and Mrs. Cirone had advised emphatically against that. It wasn't until later, when the building was completely dark and the streets outside were still, that we understood and then appreciated their wisdom and insistence.

Other things used that floor at night.

I never did pull together the nerve to open my eyes and see *what,* exactly, but I heard them. Hard-shelled things. By the thousands.

They left us alone. But I knew that I wasn't the only one to lie awake all night making sure they didn't change their minds.

Everyone woke up grumpy, but another delicious meal— eggs, black beans, tortillas, sweet bread, and a slice of papaya— and a morning spent in one of the city's plazas, doing some shopping and performing two of our skits, cheered us considerably. The air was beautifully warm and thick, alive with the smell of flowers. All around us, everyone and everything seemed vibrant with color. Women's dresses. Little boys' T-shirts. Paintings on walls and the sides of buses. Vegetables and fruit for sale. Teens in school uniforms. A man on a cement bench playing an acoustic guitar. Children selling souvenirs—wallets, T-shirts, necklaces, sombreros, baskets, statues of the virgin Mother, painted wooden bowls and vases, bottles of vanilla, blankets. Sunlight pushing through mist in the sculpted green trees and sparkling on the water in the fountain at the center of the plaza.

Color. Heat. Smells.

I didn't know if it was because I was unobservant at home or because this plaza was so different from anything I had ever experienced, but it captivated every one of my senses. From the floral pattern on a little girl's shoes and the chattering of high heels on cement to the quickness of the Spanish words spoken and the taste of sunscreen on my lips, the place, the moment, left me feeling as if I'd never be able to take it all in.

One of the things I had no trouble taking in, though, was the poverty. The houses just beyond the plaza had sheet-metal roofs and no glass or screens for their windows. Trash cluttered the streets. Most children were wearing no shoes. Beggars, many of them tiny children, tugged on my shirt, saying, "*¿Me da para un pan?*" (Can you give me money for bread?) Voices clamored around us. "*¿Quiere chicle?*" "*¿Quiere Jicama?*" "*¿Quiere naranjas?*" (Do you want gum? Do you want Jicama? Do you want oranges?) Mr. Cirone had instructed us not to give away money because doing so only kept the people needy. Even though it was difficult to see that larger picture as I looked into the eyes of the children surrounding me, I obeyed him. He had been in poor countries before. He had to know what he was talking about.

The need was so great. So overwhelming.

The realization sobered me that one of my hair clips—which I could buy without a second thought—would probably cost someone in Poza Rica a week's wages, and I couldn't help feeling uncomfortably conspicuous when, late in the morning, we climbed back into our shiny American church vans with our over-stuffed backpacks and drove south out of town.

We drove through El Chote and into El Tajin for the first of the two "sightseeing" excursions Mr. Cirone had scheduled for us. The second, a trip to the beach, would come during our drive back home.

El Tajin, the ruins of a Totonaco pyramid site, had been unearthed in the area's rugged tree-covered hills, and exploring it was both awe-inspiring and eerie. A thousand years old and completely foreign. We visited the museum at the site, watched a group of *Voladores* from Papantla perform a dance that was meant to appease the Totonaco rain god, and stopped to buy souvenirs.

Hundreds of children, it seemed, had gathered to sell vanilla, shiny black hematite jewelry, various sizes of *Palo de lluvia*—bamboo sticks capped on each end and filled with tiny beads or seashells that rattled against nails poked through the sides to make different pitches and types of sound—and other keepsakes of El Tajin. We ate lunch at a restaurant called *Enrique* and then reluctantly got back into the vans for the drive north back to Poza Rica and then west toward the end of the road at Coxquihui and the remote villages beyond it.

For three hours we curved through the jungle, *La Huasteca Veracruzana,* with more trucks than cars sharing the road with us. Mainly trucks that were overloaded and loud, chugging out foul-smelling blue-black puffs of diesel exhaust. Upon entering every village along the way, huge speed bumps—called *topes*, Mr. Cirone told us—forced us to slow to a near stop just to navigate them, leaving us vulnerable to the sickening fumes of the vehicles ahead of us.

All this gave me a horrible headache. And when the road turned from pavement to gravel, my stomach had had enough. I leaned forward and rested my head on my knees.

"People drive like maniacs around here," Mr. Cirone was saying to his wife.

"And on these roads," she replied.

"Did you see the bus off the road at that last corner we passed?"

"No," said Mrs. Cirone. "Please keep your eyes *on* the road."

A gentle touch at my shoulder startled me. And then the question, "Are you all right, Ash?"

I opened my eyes, sat up straight, and looked over at Judah. He'd moved up a seat to sit beside me. "Yeah," I said. "Just a little carsick."

Who'd have thought that my first words to Judah Ewen after two years would be about carsickness?

"You should try to sleep," he said.

Another huge truck sped by us. Close. "I don't think that's going to happen."

He smiled and nodded.

"We're going to stop soon," Mr. Cirone announced from the driver's seat. "Everyone wake up."

I wondered who he thought was sleeping!

"Starting tomorrow," he said cheerfully, "no more driving."

The thick plant life and rough terrain outside the van made me wonder if that would turn out to be as much of a blessing as it sounded right at that moment.

"Mr. Meyer is going to meet us at the first village on the trail," Mr. Cirone said. "And we'll spend a couple days there before he takes us around to all the others he ministers in."

"We're going to walk to all of them?" someone behind me asked.

"Yep."

"In the early morning, I hope?" Mrs. Cirone glanced pleadingly at her husband.

"Mostly." He grinned as he turned off the air conditioning and told us to roll down our windows.

It took all of two minutes for the van to become almost unbearably hot and humid.

"Whew." Judah wiped sweat from his upper lip with his forearm.

I did the same.

"We're going to die," Hope whispered.

"Nah," said one of the boys. Shane. From Georgia. "You get used to it."

"*You* do, maybe," Callie replied. "I'm from Minnesota, remember?"

"How about me?" I moaned. "I'm from Alaska!"

"You'll get used to it," Shane insisted, laughing. "Don't think about the heat. Think about how good it smells." He inhaled deeply. "I bet y'all don't get smells like this in Alaska and Minnesota."

When I breathed in, all I could smell was *wet*. Like freshly mowed grass after rain. Wet dirt. Wet green. Wet wood. But there was a sweetness to the air that I hadn't experienced before, and I took a few minutes to enjoy it.

Hope, however, began to sneeze.

Mr. Cirone chuckled. "Yes. I did pack allergy stuff."

"We're going to die," Hope said again. Dramatically.

Everyone laughed.

But by the time we slowed to enter the village, our laughter had been smothered by heat and the exhaust fumes from the colorfully painted bus ahead of us.

Most of the buildings in this area seemed to be constructed of nailed-together wooden planks with rusted corrugated tin roofs, many having no glass or screens in the windows—only crude curtains. But there were also cement buildings with tin, asbestos, or flat concrete roofs, some of them painted white from the roof down to the bottom edge of the windows and red-brown below that to the ground. Mr. Cirone told us that this was done to obscure the mud splashes of the rainy season and enabled the buildings to look cleaner longer.

Eventually, we arrived in the plaza. Though much smaller than Poza Rica, this village seemed just as alive and busy. A Catholic church stood at one corner. A hotel. Houses. Markets. Along one of the streets running into the plaza, tarps and canvases had been strung from roof to roof, shading the tarps spread out on the street below where vendors displayed their merchandise. Matches. Irons. Shoes. Pots. Fruits. Tape players. Clothing. Toys.

Other small stands lined the perimeter of the plaza. A *paleteria*—an ice-cream shop. A *carniceria*—a meat market. A couple of *tortillerias* and *panaderias*—tortilla and bread stands. Taco stands. Many of the signs above the tables had the names of saints written on them . . . *Fruteria San Gabriel,* a fruit stand. I noticed significantly fewer vendors selling souvenirs in this village than in the plaza at Poza Rica and more vendors selling witchcraft items—like statues of the female idol *La Santisima Muerte* (The Sacred Death) and alum crystals which, when thrown into fire, were supposed to release spirits, as well as many herbal potions for curses, blessings, and so forth.

Mr. Cirone parked his van beside a hotel, and Mr. Marsh pulled up behind him. When we'd checked into our rooms and unloaded the vans, Mr. Cirone said, "You can look around the plaza, if you like. Free time till dinner. Just stay in groups of two or more and don't go outside of the square." He glanced at his watch. "Be back here by 6:00 to eat."

Mr. Marsh had told us that most Mexican cities, towns, and villages had been built around a central plaza. A community place for local events, once-a-week markets, festivals, and so on. *The Quiosco*—a platform in the plaza—was the place in each village where we would perform our skits and hand out tracts and New Testaments printed in Spanish.

Rebekah and I started walking away from the hotel. As partners, we'd agreed to always stay together. "I want to go look inside the church," I said. "Do you mind?"

"Nope." She smiled. "Maybe it'll be cooler inside."

Someone ran up behind us. Rebekah and I turned at the same time to see who it was.

"Mr. Cirone asked us to go with you two," Shane said, pointing at Judah who was coming up slowly behind him.

I shrugged. Rebekah glanced questioningly from Judah to me.

"What?" Shane asked. "Is there a problem?"

"No," I said. "No. Thanks."

So the four of us walked to the church and entered through a huge open wooden door.

Shane led the way slowly around a small partition as our eyes adjusted to the dimness inside.

"It's beautiful," I whispered.

We walked up the side aisle toward the altar and sat in one of the front pews.

"It seems strange to see gold in here when everyone out there is so poor." Judah was clearly not as interested in the architecture and adornment of the church as I was. In fact, he seemed almost offended by it.

I looked at a statue of the current pope to the left of the altar and then at a statue of Jesus to the right. There was a statue of the virgin Mary, center stage. I looked at the many tall golden candle stands. At the iron crucifix with Jesus still on it. At the embroidered cloth covering the table where a huge Bible sat open beside a gold cup with a small white cloth draped over its lip. At a staff with something gold at its end that looked like the sun the way a child might draw. At the table of red candles, many of them lit and burning, below the altar. At the mosaics of Joseph, Mary, and the Baby Jesus, all with golden haloes, on the walls on either side of the crucifix. Walls trimmed with gold.

"I wonder when this church was built," I said. "Was it a mission?"

Judah stood up and stepped past me. "I'm going to wait outside."

After he disappeared behind the wooden partition, Rebekah leaned toward me and said, "He just doesn't appreciate beautiful art."

"It isn't meant to just be art," Shane pointed out.

I nodded thoughtfully. "I guess we shouldn't leave him waiting too long."

We met Judah at the bottom of the steps in front of the church and started walking slowly around the perimeter of the plaza. We wanted to see, hear, and experience everything. We explored some of the fruit and vegetable stands. We stopped at a table where Shane bought a necklace for his sister. We entered another building that looked to be a Protestant church of some kind, but we found nobody there.

As we stepped back into the sunshine outside and started walking down the front steps, I noticed a table of leather goods about halfway down the first block of one of the streets going out of the plaza. Wallets. Shoes. Jackets. "Let's go look over there," I suggested.

Judah shook his head. "We're not supposed to leave the plaza."

"Oh . . . that's right." I stared longingly at the table. "But I'd love to find a handcrafted wallet for my dad."

"I guess it'd be okay," Shane said to Judah. "I'll take her, and you and Rebekah can wait here."

"You'll be able to see us the whole time," I added . . . feeling that I needed Judah's approval somehow. Probably because I knew he was right. We weren't supposed to leave the plaza.

But what could it hurt, really? The table wasn't even twenty yards from where we were standing.

I hesitated for only a moment before walking quickly toward the table with Shane.

Chapter 5

"These are just the kind my dad likes," I said to Shane as I leaned over the table to look more closely at one of the wallets. I'd been standing there several minutes and still hadn't decided on one to buy. "They're all so nice . . ."

"Just pick one," Shane urged.

I laughed. Boys did not understand the art of shopping.

"Come on, Ashton," he pressed. "We're not supposed to be here, remember?"

"Yeah. Yeah, I remember." Quickly, I narrowed my choices down to my two favorite wallets and then pointed at each while asking Shane which one he liked best.

Clearly uninterested in either, he chose one.

I selected the other, pulled my wallet out of my waist pack, and paid the vendor behind the table. "Thanks," I said. "*Gracias.*"

The man nodded as he placed Dad's wallet into a plastic bag and handed it, and my change, back to me.

Shane turned back toward the plaza. "Let's go."

"Okay, okay." I zipped my change into my wallet and dropped it into the sack. Just to tease Shane, I said, "You know, now that I think about it, I guess I did like the one you picked better. Do you think they'd let me exchange it?"

"Don't even think about it," he said. His tone was testy until he saw my smile.

OUT OF HIDING

As we walked toward Judah and Rebekah, I allowed myself to swing my sack at my side a little more vigorously than would have been necessary. I'd bought my wallet. Without incident. Yes, we'd left the plaza for a few minutes, but everything was fine. Judah had always been the one to follow every rule in every circumstance, and . . .

. . . and that's why he wasn't with Tommy when he drowned. He'd stayed on the trail, as they'd been told to do. Tommy had taken the shortcut.

The satisfaction of the moment was quickly replaced by a tight feeling I couldn't have named, and my sack hung at my side. "I'm sorry I made you break the rules, Shane," I said.

"You didn't make me do anything." He smiled. "But I've got to tell you, if I'd known what a slow shopper you—*hey!*"

At his shout, I felt a tug at my hand, and my sack was gone. The wallet for Dad. And *my* wallet! "All my money's in there," I yelled as I turned to see the back of a boy running past the table and farther down the street away from the plaza.

Shane took off after the boy and, a moment later, so did Judah.

"Stop!" I called to them. "It's not worth—"

But they didn't stop.

I looked over my shoulder at Rebekah. She was already running back across the plaza toward our hotel. I turned and ran the same way Shane and Judah had gone. I had to catch them before anything bad happened. I followed them. Straight up the street, around a corner, and onto another street. I noticed the buildings I was passing, cement like those in the plaza, but not as white. I noticed the stray dogs, the black hairy pigs, and the mules. I noticed the men who whistled at me as I ran by them. And I noticed that I could no longer hear the calls of the vendors in the plaza, but I kept running. Kept following.

The farther we went from the plaza, the farther apart and more run-down the buildings were.

"Shane!" I yelled. "Judah?"

I'd come to a Y in the street, and I didn't know which way they had gone.

I stopped running, suddenly frightened.

Where were they?

Where was I?

Resolved not to panic, I determined that the only thing to do was head back toward the plaza. Even though we'd made a couple of turns from the street that would get me there, I was sure I'd be able to find it.

I turned and started walking.

With every step away from that Y in the road, the muscles in my shoulders tightened. Tears pressed at my eyes, but I refused to let them surface. Why had I insisted on leaving the plaza? Where were Judah and Shane now? What if something happens to one of them? What if—-

I heard footsteps in the dirt behind me. I spun around, hoping to see Judah and Shane.

But it wasn't them.

Three boys approached me. They started grinning and calling things out to me. Things I couldn't understand . . . except *bonita, gringa,* and *dia.* Beautiful. White girl. Day. Their tone was not one of helpfulness, so I turned and kept walking. More quickly than I had been.

The boys followed and caught up with me. They just teased at first, but then one of them grabbed me.

I screamed.

The boys began to shove me. Back and forth between them. Laughing. Whistling. Asking me questions I couldn't understand.

"¿De donde eres?"

"¿Cual de nosotros te gusta mas?"

"¿Eres de los evangelicos, verdad?"

What would they do when they got bored with shoving me around?

I yelled, "Somebody help me!" But I had run so far from the plaza, and Judah and Shane could be half a mile away by now. Who would help me? I could be killed in this street, and nobody might ever find me or know what happened.

Suddenly, the boy nearest me yelled out in pain and stumbled backward. I didn't know why. I didn't care. This was my chance, and I took it.

I pushed right between the other two boys and ran.

"Ashton! Go get Mr. Cirone!"

I turned at Judah's voice, just in time to see one of the boys smack him across the back of the neck with a plank of wood. Judah went to his hands and knees, and the other two boys piled into him, kicking, punching, yelling. Suddenly Shane was there too, yanking one of the boys away from Judah.

And then there was a man's voice behind me. Right behind me. " *¡Javier! ¡Pablo! ¡Dejenlo! No quiero que vuelvan a meternos en problemas con los judiciales.*"

All three boys instantly got to their feet and stepped away from Shane and Judah, their expressions turning so quickly and completely to fearful that nobody would have believed them capable of the violence they had been enjoying only moments before.

"¡Dejenlo ir ya!"

Without hesitation the boys ran between two houses, off the street and out of sight.

I turned quickly, unnerved.

At first glance, I wondered how the man could have inspired such fear in the three boys. He was thin and elderly, and barely taller than I was. But then I noticed a ragged scar coming down from the outside corner of his left eye, and his angry stare, and his steady eyes. Plain and simple, he looked mean. And the way he allowed me to absorb that meanness—for just an instant before walking away . . . .

"Ashton? Are you all right?" asked Judah.

I turned quickly, grateful to be putting that man behind me again.

Judah stood slowly, rubbing the back of his neck as I approached him. Was that blood on his hand?

I placed my hand on his arm. "Yeah," I said. "I'm all right. Are you?"

He nodded and then turned to Shane. "You?"

Shane wiped at his nose, which was beginning to bleed. "I'm fine," he said. "We couldn't get your stuff, Ashton. Sorry. The kid was too fast, and he knew where he was going. We lost him."

"I don't care," I said. "It's just money."

"Did you have anything else in your wallet?" Judah asked me.

I shook my head. "All my important stuff is in my pouch." I tapped at my stomach where the pouch Mr. Cirone had given me was strapped beneath my shirt. "It was just money and a few pictures in my wallet."

"That's good," Judah said.

I agreed, even though it was *all* of my money. "I'm just glad you guys are okay," I said quietly, "and that you got back here when you did! We never should have left the plaza."

And I had promised my father that I'd be careful, that I would obey the rules. My stomach hurt.

"We better get back," Judah said. "Mr. Cirone will want an explanation."

"He's not going to like it," I muttered, thinking again how foolish I had been to leave the plaza. "The whole thing is my fault. I'll tell him."

Shane laughed a little. "It's not going to make any difference who tells him."

Glancing frequently over our shoulders, we started walking back toward the street that led to the plaza.

When we got back to the plaza, Mr. Cirone and Mr. Marsh were waiting for us.

I swallowed hard and tried to hide my nervousness when they led us to the hotel, to the door to the Cirones' room—past all the other kids who were trying (but failing) not to look at us—and stepped aside to let us in. Judah sat heavily on one of the five chairs at the room's corner table. I sat beside him. Shane beside me. Even though the table was round and the chairs were spaced fairly evenly around it, it felt as if Judah and Shane and I were on one side of a huge, empty pastor's desk, and Mr. Cirone and Mr. Marsh were on the other. The Pastor's side.

"We're going to pray," said Mr. Cirone, "and then you three are going to talk." He smiled. "And then it's my turn."

Intimidating, but deserved. I bowed my head.

After mumbling an *amen* to Mr. Cirone's prayer, I opened my eyes and started talking. I had promised to be the one to tell him why we'd left the plaza, and that's exactly what I did. When I finished, I stared down at the tabletop and waited.

"Well, Miss Cook," Mr. Cirone said finally, "I think we're all thankful that this wasn't a more costly lesson."

"Yes, sir."

"From now on you'll keep to the rules?"

I nodded. I would.

So would Judah. So would Shane.

"All right, then." Mr. Cirone stood. "We'll see what we can do about your wallet, Ashton, but I wouldn't count on getting it back."

"Okay," I said. "Thanks."

"Go get cleaned up. You've got half an hour or so before we have dinner and then head to the plaza for our performance there."

I stepped outside ahead of Judah and Shane and walked slowly back to my room, cringing against the heat of the early evening sun on my shoulders and back. It had already been a very long day, and it was going to be difficult, after all that had just happened, to focus on the opportunity ahead of me to minister to people in the plaza. All I wanted to do was go to bed for the night.

But that was not an option.

A shower, however, was.

I muttered *hellos* to the other three girls when I walked into the room, but hurried into the bathroom before anyone could say anything back to me. I needed to relax. I needed to wash the dirty handprints from my arms. I needed to pray that God would still use me even though I'd been so stupid. But roaches turned my shower into a breath-grabbing, foot-shaking experience.

Yuck! Stuff was supposed to go down the drain, not come up it!

Afterwards, I apologized to Rebekah for being so insistent about getting that wallet for my father—a wallet I didn't have now, anyway. She accepted the apology and quickly directed the conversation to other things. Nothing things. After a while, Mr. Cirone knocked on our door—rounding up the team for dinner. Tacos—ground *chorizo* (pork sausage), chilies, sautéed onions, and cilantro in two small fresh tortillas—bought from a reputable vendor in the plaza. And warm soda served to us in plastic bags.

Matt shook his taco in the air after taking a couple of bites. "These are good," he said.

Mr. Marsh chuckled. "Don't sound so surprised. Do you think Americans are the only people who like to enjoy their food?"

"What about the *mole?*" someone challenged, inspiring an instant and unanimous groan from the rest of us.

"Well . . . some tastes are acquired."

When everyone had finished eating, Mr. Cirone sent three of the boys into the plaza to tell people about our performance. The rest of us gathered there to pray and wait. Mr. Cirone had assured us that we'd never lack an audience—being Americans, we were naturally a curiosity. On this night, in this village, his words proved to be true. In fact, so many people assembled around us that I began to feel nervous . . . especially when I noticed the group of boys who had grabbed me earlier standing with several somewhat hostile-looking men. They were older men, dressed in white, glaring at us with their arms folded across their chests, their eyes narrow and unyielding, daring us to impress them. I looked for the man who had chased the boys away from us, but I didn't see him.

Should I point the boys out to Mr. Cirone? They should get in trouble for what they had done. And what of the boy who'd stolen my sack? He could be in the crowd too, and I'd never know it. Nobody had gotten a good look at his face.

"Buenas tardes," Mr. Cirone shouted. He spoke to the quieting crowd in Spanish for several seconds, telling them who we were, and then introduced Chad, who stepped out into the open square and held up a plain wood cross.

I'd have to wait until afterwards to do anything about the three boys.

We began the skit. While Mr. Cirone narrated in Spanish, we silently acted out different responses to Chad as he mingled among us offering his cross. Some of us mocked the cross and pushed it away. Others followed Chad around but never reached forward for the cross. Others clasped onto the cross and then joined Chad in trying to share it. After Mr. Cirone had made the point to the crowd that Chad's cross represented more than just a religion—it stood for life in Christ—we began the last part of the skit. Even though the event we were about to enact was certain to be familiar to everyone watching, we knew that its life-giving *reality* was not.

The Crucifixion.

I had been assigned a role as one of those who'd demanded Jesus' death. During our practices in Texas, it hadn't bothered me to pretend to shout at "Jesus," to shake my fist at Him, and spit at

Him because He was just *Chad*, my friend from home. One of the guys on our mission team. Not really Jesus. But here in Mexico . . . he was still just an actor, not really Jesus, and yet . . .

Maybe it was the intense attention of the people all around me. Or maybe it was because I had been confronted earlier that afternoon with my own imperfection and disobedience. Or maybe it was the simple fact that this wasn't a practice, but an actual presentation of the gospel. Whatever the reason . . . I could not bring myself to raise my hand when "Jesus" walked by me as Mr. Cirone shouted "*¡Crucifiquenlo! ¡Crucifiquenlo!*"

Crucify Him.

All I could do was move to join the kids who had been assigned parts as followers of Jesus, kneel with them, and weep with them when two of the boys laid "Jesus" on the ground, stretched out his arms, and pretended to hammer nails into his wrists.

At the end of our presentation—after an enactment of the Resurrection and an "altar call" from Mr. Cirone—I found a bench out of the way of the people coming forward and the members of our team who were praying with them. I bowed my head and prayed silently for those receiving Christ . . . and for myself.

By the time I finished, the plaza had grown nearly dark with the setting of the sun, and most of the people had left.

Including, I noticed, the three boys who had attacked me.

Chapter 6

I stood in front of the mirror in our hotel room early the next morning, adjusting the shoulder straps on my backpack. We had already eaten breakfast and were getting ready to leave for the village—a seven-mile hike through the jungle—where we'd meet up with Dane Meyer. I'd pulled my hair up and back in a loose French braid and had put on jeans and my white cotton shirt.

It should be an easy day. Hot—already, at just over an hour past sunrise, the temperature was 85 degrees—but easy.

Judging by the moaning and grunting going on behind me, though, as Hope and Rebekah labored to settle into their packs, I was the only one who thought so.

"I'm going to die," Hope said. "They honestly expect us to walk seven miles with these things?"

Rebekah nodded. "And it's going to be so hot."

Callie laughed. "What a couple of babies."

"Oh, listen to Miss Mountain Woman," Hope muttered.

"You just have to pace yourselves," I said, hoping to deaden the sting of Callie's comment. But it didn't work.

Though Hope and Rebekah said nothing, their faces made it clear enough that they didn't appreciate the criticism.

"You guys shouldn't have been whining, is all," Callie said quietly. "I'm sorry." Then she walked by us on her way out the door.

I followed her. "Callie, wait up."

She stopped walking but didn't turn to face me.

"Have you done a lot of hiking?" I asked her when I'd caught up to her. Perhaps that would explain her irritability somehow. Experienced people sometimes lacked patience with beginners—especially "whining" ones.

"No," she said. "It's just . . . they shouldn't have been complaining. They knew what we'd be doing when they signed up to come. If they thought it was going to be so awful, they should have stayed home."

She had a point, sort of.

She pushed her hand back through her hair, stared up at the sky for a moment, and let out a long breath. "I'm sorry, Ashton," she said. "I always blurt out stuff without thinking. Lately, anyway. It just makes me so mad when people whose lives are probably perfect complain about stuff." She paused. "They don't know what real problems are."

"You don't know that," I reminded her.

She neither agreed nor disagreed. "Anyway," she said, "I'm sorry for what I said."

"I wasn't offended," I assured her. "But, then, your comment wasn't aimed at me."

She nodded and walked slowly back toward the hotel.

Most of the boys were outside already, comparing the height and size of their packs and discussing their hiking boots—which brand was the most rugged, and so on. I smiled as I sat on a bench beside Chad. "That was pretty powerful last night. All the people coming up for prayer." I let my pack rest against the wall behind us and leaned against it.

"Ash," he said, looking right at me, "I stayed awake all night thinking about what happened to you, Shane, and Ewen yesterday."

That was the last thing I wanted to talk about. Especially with Chad Reese. I knew he'd find some way to tie yesterday's events to Tommy's death.

Chad had never liked Judah. Three boys had always seemed one too many, and Chad had usually been the one to leave, angry and feeling excluded. When Tommy died, Chad had been one of the first people to blame Judah to his face. Coldly. Horribly. "Chad, I—"

"Why did he break the rules to run after Shane yesterday, for a bag of souvenirs and money, when he wouldn't break the rules to go with Tommy?"

"I don't know, Chad." I stared down at my knees. I couldn't say that the question hadn't occurred to me during the night, but I'd refused to give it any room in my thinking. I stood, adjusted my pack, and stepped away from Chad. "Maybe he learned something that day at the river. I don't know. I do know I didn't come here to think about Tommy." I looked down at Chad. "Okay?"

"How can you *not* think about him when you have to look at Ewen every day?" He shook his head. "It's been all I could do to not—"

"Yeah, well just keep on not doing it. Okay? This isn't the place."

He stared right at me for several long seconds. "That's your trick, isn't it?" he asked, finally, quietly. "It's been your trick all along. 'If I don't think about it, it'll be okay.'"

I didn't know how to answer him, or whether or not he even expected me to. "This isn't the place to start thinking about it," I repeated. "That's all I'm saying." I turned and walked away from him before he could say any more. I'd worked so hard to raise the money for this trip and had looked forward to it so much. I would not experience it angry. If Chad was right, and I had survived Tommy's death only because I'd refused to think about it . . . well, I could think about it later. After I got home. Or maybe not at all. Not thinking about it was better than being angry and hateful all the time—wasn't it?

I found Shane standing near a tree and joined him. "How's the nose?" I asked.

"Fine." He smiled. "It's the eye that's bugging me."

His right eye was bruised at the corner and had swollen enough to prevent him from opening it fully.

"I'm sorry, Shane," I said.

He waved away the apology. "How long have you been a Christian?" he asked me.

I squinted at him, curious. Talk about changing the subject! Then I shrugged. "Since kindergarten, I guess." I began rolling and unrolling the loose end of my belt.

"Me too," he said. Then he reconsidered. "Well, that's how long I've known Jesus as my Savior. I've only recently started thinking of Him as my Lord too."

I nodded, then pointed at his hiking boots. "Those look like they'd take you anywhere." I knew what he'd meant about making Jesus his Lord. I even understood it . . . the difference. I just didn't want to talk about it. "Have you been backpacking before?"

"Yeah," he said, "but not in this kind of heat."

Even with the sun still fairly low, the air was stagnant with heat and thick with the feel of rain. But the sky was cloudless. "I'm sure we'll rest a lot."

"Not too much, I hope." Shane squinted up at the sun. "The earlier in the day we get there, the better."

Judah approached us then, carrying his pack in his hands rather than on his back. He stood beside Shane.

"You look awful," Shane said to him.

"I didn't sleep." He tried to smile. "I bought one of those snow-cone things last night, and it didn't agree with me."

Shane laughed and slapped Judah's back. "Victim number one!"

Judah pulled away from Shane's hand. "I'm moved by your concern."

"Are you all right to hike?" Shane asked.

"I'm fine."

Ten minutes later, when Hope, Callie, and Rebekah finally emerged from our hotel room, packs and new hats on, Mr. Cirone gathered us all together for a word of prayer and some last-minute instructions about which plants we could and could not touch. When he finished, he and his wife led the way across the plaza and along one of the streets, which eventually narrowed to our trail in the jungle.

We walked single file. Mr. Cirone. Mrs. Cirone. Three of the boys. Rebekah. Me. Hope. Callie. The other three boys. Mr. Marsh. Nobody spoke much. The uneven terrain and the increasing heat of the morning demanded our full attention. I didn't regret my choice of wearing jeans. The abundant plant life didn't exactly respect the boundary of the trail and slapped frequently against the front of my legs.

As hot as the air was, and though my back began to ache from ducking under so many branches, the jungle captivated me. Especially its *green*. Ferns huge enough to shade one of our vans. Giant trees—trees with leaves of every size, shape, and color.

After about an hour, half of which had been consistently uphill, Mr. Cirone announced a break. Most of the kids shed their packs, sat down, and reached instantly for their canteens. I didn't. I found a tree to lean back against, slid my shoulder straps off my shoulders, and stood, leaning against my pack while I took my drink. Not too much. Just a few mouthfuls. There was nothing worse than trying to hike with a stomach full of water.

"How far have we come?" Shane asked Mr. Cirone.

"Two and a quarter miles, maybe."

"Oh," Hope moaned. "I'm going to die!"

Everyone laughed. But only briefly.

I noticed, as I stood there, that Hope, Callie, and Rebekah seemed to have resolved their earlier conflict and had no difficulty in finding things to talk and laugh about. I decided to leave them to it for a while.

Maybe I could join the boys' conversation.

I'd always felt more at ease with boys than girls. Probably because I had an older brother and had always done things with him. Things that most girls seemed to hate. Backpacking. Four-wheel driving. Fishing. I didn't wear make-up. I didn't enjoy squealing about boys. I didn't count fat grams. I loved to rough it and never whined about having to wash my hair in freezing-cold lake water with that biodegradable shampoo that could also be used for toothpaste, dish soap, lure cleaner, and to get engine grease or the smell of horse sweat out of your clothes.

I hoisted my pack back onto my shoulders, bounced it around until it settled into a comfortable position, and walked down the trail toward them.

Judah stood when he saw me coming and offered me the piece of fallen log he had been sitting on.

"That's okay," I said. "I'd rather stand." But the comment sounded more rude than honest—even though it was honest—so I added, "You look like you need the seat more than I do." That didn't sound much better, I realized, but it was true too. "How are you feeling?" I asked him.

"I'm okay."

He didn't look okay. "We *were* warned about buying food from just any vendor," I reminded him.

"I know."

I said, "So, was it worth it? The snow cone?"

"No. Definitely not." He looked up at me. "Do you remember that—"

"Don't even get into the Disgusting Food Memories recital, Judah." I raised my hand to stop him.

But he knew that he need only mouth the words *Blackened Trout* to force me to defend myself by reminding him of the time he and Tommy had tried to barbecue a frozen pizza when power was out at the lake after a storm. And "barbecue" was exactly what resulted. He mouthed the words. I retaliated. He responded with another of my failed adventures in cooking. I mentioned his campfire Blueberry Goo, which was supposed to be pancakes except that Mrs. Ewen had forgotten to pack a spatula.

"I came to truly appreciate granola bars on that trip," I said. "The Breakfast of the Utensil-less."

He nodded.

I suspected, in the uncomfortable silence that followed as the smiles slowly left both of our faces, that we were thinking the same things. How we'd had so many good times together. How it had ended.

"I'm sure Mr. Marsh would go back with you if you're feeling too sick to make it another five miles," I said.

"I'm okay."

"Okay, then." I turned away from him.

"Ash?"

I stopped walking, but didn't face him.

"I . . . we . . . never mind."

Never mind I could do. I walked back up the trail and stood beside Mr. Marsh while the others lamented their stiff muscles as they stood and got back into their packs. By not sitting down, I had spared myself that agony.

Mr. Marsh nodded toward Judah. "Is he feeling any better?" he asked me.

"I don't think so."

"Do you know how they make those so-called snow cones, Miss Cook?"

"No."

"They buy big blocks of ice—frozen untreated water—shave it off in little shards, and pour fruit-colored syrup over it. Like a snow cone back home . . . except for what it does to your stomach. An experience you'll never forget."

Untreated water.

Mr. Marsh watched Judah for several seconds. He was visibly concerned, but didn't say anything to him.

"Let's go," Mr. Cirone called out. He stepped back onto the trail and led the way deeper into the jungle. Jumping from rock to rock along a riverbed. "We'll stop for lunch," he promised.

"So, Ashton," Hope said from behind me after a while, "do you have a boyfriend?"

"No."

"Do you like anyone?"

"No."

She stayed silent a moment. "How about you, Callie?"

"His name's Cole."

"Tell us about him."

Callie sighed. "Later. When we're not walking. I need all the breath I can get just to stay on my feet!"

"Know what you mean," Hope said. "How about you, Rebekah?"

"No. I don't have a boyfriend."

"Do you like someone?"

"What are you?" I asked Hope, teasing, "the youth mission gossip columnist?"

She laughed. "Just curious. Trying to get my mind off the growing blister on my left little toe. So . . . do you like someone?"

Oh, brother.

"I guess," Rebekah admitted.

"What's his name?"

No answer.

"Why aren't you dating?"

"Because . . . he doesn't want to yet."

"Hmm." Silence. Then, "Yet?"

Rebekah laughed. "Hope, give it a rest. He's going away to college in the fall and thinks that dating at this point will make things more complicated for us than they have to be."

"Sounds like you don't share the sentiment."

"So now she's the youth mission analyst too." I grinned.

"That's right. Rebekah?"

"I . . . don't want to talk about this right now."

"Please don't," one of the boys in front of her—was it Judah?—muttered.

From the head of the line came a loud, clear, and unmistakably insistent, "Amen!"

"Thank you, Mr. Cirone." Rebekah laughed. "So very much."

Through the increasing heat of mid- and late-morning, we walked. In silence, for the most part, except for the occasional complaint about a branch in the face or a root in the trail. The heat was merciless. And draining.

Everyone was grateful when Mr. Cirone finally stopped us for lunch.

Whew. Hot.

I dropped my pack in the shade of a tree and sat beside it.

Mr. Cirone tossed a package of crackers and squeeze cheese to each of us. "Eat up," he said. "It's only another mile or so . . . but lots of uphill."

A simultaneous and unanimous groan expressed our opinion well enough.

Mr. Cirone chuckled. He didn't even look winded!

"Aren't you dying, Hope?" Shane asked as he sat beside her.

She smiled up at him. "I'm too tired to die."

As Rebekah sat beside me, and Judah beside her, she said, "I'm going to lose ten pounds."

"You might gain weight," I told her. "Muscle is heavier than fat."

Both Judah and Rebekah looked at me as if they couldn't believe I'd just said that.

"Hey," I stammered, "I didn't mean . . ."

"It's okay."

"No, Rebekah, I didn't mean—"

She chuckled . . . sort of. "It's not a problem."

I left it alone. I'd probably only stick my foot in my mouth again if I kept talking. Why did everything suddenly feel so awkward?

We sat in the shade for nearly an hour . . . not that the shade was all that cool. It wasn't. But the rest refreshed me enough that the prospect of hiking that last mile seemed significantly less daunting.

"Let's go," Mr. Cirone said. "Mr. Ewen, you'll walk with me."

Everyone looked at Judah as he shoved his unopened crackers and cheese into one of his pack's side pouches, lifted his pack onto his back, and slowly walked to the head of the line to join Mr. Cirone.

Hope stepped onto the trail behind me. "That snow cone he ate better have tasted good."

"I'm going to go walk with him," Rebekah said. Taking care about her footing in the plants to the left side of the trail, Rebekah walked by me, the three boys ahead of me, and Mrs. Cirone to take the place in line right behind Judah.

Mr. Cirone glanced curiously around his pack at her, but said nothing.

Hope, however, said, "Hmm."

We walked.

Uphill.

Uphill that was relentless and tedious, and frighteningly close to vertical. In many places we had to use our hands as well as our feet. Climbing. Right hand. Left foot. Right foot. Left hand.

I had never sweated so much in my life.

The jungle was like a huge sauna with no door.

Finally, though, the terrain leveled, and we began to pass lean-tos in the trees. Women looked up at us from where they were crushing chilies in huge bowls with stone pestles—*molcajete*. Children wearing stretched and dingy white T-shirts, shorts, and no shoes stopped playing to stare at us, their eyes wide and curious. Mr. Cirone greeted them in Spanish. None of them replied; in fact, many ran from him.

The trail widened as we walked, and it eventually opened into a primitive version of a plaza. Mr. Cirone led us toward a pile of building materials. Poles from Chijol trees, *orcones*. Yellow-green bamboo-type poles, *tarro*. Some firmer bamboo poles, *carizo*. Next to them were several heaps of cut vines, *bejuco*, to secure the bamboo poles in place for the walls. Palm leaves for the thatched roof. And the stones which we would mix with mud to make *cimiento* for the church's foundation.

This was where we'd meet Dane Meyer.

With Mr. Cirone's permission, we gratefully dropped our packs, leaning them upright against the piles of building materials, while he walked to the small stick building just behind the site and tapped on its loosely hung front door.

"Didn't Mr. Meyer know what day we were coming?" one of the kids asked nobody in particular.

"Must be siesta time."

"Sounds like a good idea to me!"

Hope nodded as she sat heavily beside her pack. "This time, I really *am* going to die."

Afraid I'd never get back up if I sat down, and knowing that Mr. Cirone would be back any minute telling us we had to go somewhere or do something, I walked toward Judah. He seemed to be struggling to get out of his pack, so I stepped in behind him and offered to help.

"Thanks," he said.

I held the pack for him while he pulled his arms free of the straps and then lowered it to the ground.

"What are you doing, Ashton?"

I recognized Chad's voice behind me and hated to turn around. But I did. "Just giving him a hand," I said.

Chad glared at me. Then he muttered, "It's like you're going out of your way to be nice to him, or something!"

"I'm just being a Christian, Chad. Maybe you should try it."

Chad stomped away, but not before he made sure I got a good look at his accusing eyes . . . *You're betraying your brother, Ashton.* I ignored him and turned back to Judah.

"Thanks," he said again. And there was nothing else for either of us to say.

Several yards away from us, though, I noticed Mr. Marsh pointing in our direction and saying quite a bit to Chad.

Great, I thought. How was Chad going to explain away such visible anger without getting into the truth about all that was between him, Judah, and me?

I could only hope that he would be quick enough to shrug and mutter something about the heat and that Mr. Marsh would buy it. There was no reason for Tommy's death or anything that had happened since then to be part of this mission trip. None. It was nobody else's business. It should be left alone. Forgotten. Buried.

Mr. Cirone walked by us just then. "Dane's not there," he said.

"So . . . what do we do?" his wife asked him.

And for that moment, anyway, Chad had escaped having to explain anything to Mr. Marsh.

"Matt and I will go ask around," Mr. Cirone said. "The rest of you can go in Dane's house and take a breather."

But who will they ask? I wondered, looking out across the plaza. People had been standing and sitting, selling and buying, all around it when we'd walked into the village. And now it was empty . . . except for a few unmanned tables of items for sale.

Chapter 7

I lay on my back on top of my sleeping bag between Hope and Rebekah on the cool dirt floor of Dane Meyer's house, unable to sleep. The room was dark enough, but not quiet enough. Along with some snoring and the relaxed breathing of everyone else in the room, the noise from the jungle on the other side of the walls seemed loud, and close, and even threatening.

Why couldn't I sleep? The hike today had been exhausting. So had finding something to eat for dinner in an empty plaza—where all the vendors had disappeared. Matt and Mr. Cirone couldn't find anyone to tell them where Mr. Meyer might be. Every person they had seen had run from them.

Strange. And scary.

But Mr. and Mrs. Cirone didn't seem particularly concerned. Apparently, Mr. Meyer had mentioned to them in a letter that he was often greeted with suspicion when he visited such remote villages. In the morning, we'd get back on the trail and head to the next village—another four miles. Perhaps Mr. Meyer had been delayed there.

No big deal.

So . . . why couldn't I sleep?

Beside me, Hope rolled onto her side, pulled her knees up to her stomach, and moaned in her sleep. But then, suddenly, she was awake, getting to her hands and knees and then her feet, and bolting for the door. I could hear her outside, throwing up.

I got up, stepped more carefully over people than Hope had, pushed the door open, and whispered, "Hope?"

"Over here," she said.

"Are you all right?"

She shook her head as she used her sleeve to wipe her mouth.

"Let's get back inside."

She nodded and let me help her. She fell asleep again, but woke up sick two more times before morning, shivering with cold, then flushed and sweating hot, and then shivering again.

And she wasn't the only one.

Five people, including Mr. Marsh, spent the remaining hours of that long night running in and out to Mr. Meyer's outhouse.

"It must have been the water in Dane's water jug," Mr. Cirone said early the next morning. "I shouldn't have assumed it'd be okay." He smiled. "I'm glad it went empty before all of us could drink from it."

Those who drank from it seemed to be feeling better now, as long as they didn't move too much.

"I guess we'll hang around here today," Mr. Cirone said.

"Good," Hope said, "because there's no way I'm hiking four miles right now. I don't know how Judah did seven yesterday."

Chad rolled onto his back and stared blankly at the ceiling— at too many flies. "I feel like I got trampled by a horse."

"You look like it too." Smiling, Rebekah handed him a glass of water. Water from one of our canteens, this time. It might be old, tepid, and stale with the taste of plastic, but it would be safe.

"I'll go see if I can round up some breakfast."

When Mr. Cirone left, and after Rebekah, Callie, and I had done everything we could think of to make Chad, Hope, and the others comfortable, we walked outside together and stood in the almost cool shade at the side of Mr. Meyer's house.

"It's actually beautiful out here this time of day," Rebekah said.

I agreed. It was beautiful.

"The plaza's quiet again. That's so weird."

Rebekah leaned against the side of the house. "At home," she said, "I sleep in whenever I can. I always thought my mom was crazy when she'd say that morning is her favorite part of the day. But it really is peaceful . . . even with all that's going on."

I thought of my mother. An early riser also.

Callie walked away from us, sat on the bench in front of the window, and started to cry. She tried to hide it by turning toward the trees, but both Rebekah and I had seen her tears.

Rebekah was the first to approach her. "Callie?" She sat beside her on the bench and placed her hand on Callie's shoulder. "What's wrong?"

"It's just . . . stuff reminds me of her when I'm not expecting it, and I . . ." She breathed in deeply, wiped at her nose with a tissue she dug out of her back pocket, and looked at us. "My mom died right after Easter. I keep wondering if I'm ever going to get a grip on all these feelings that catch me off guard. I get mad, or I cry, or . . ." She shook her head. "I'm sorry."

Rebekah put her arm around Callie's shoulders.

"I probably shouldn't have even come on this trip," Callie said. "It's too soon. But it was what Mom wanted." She paused. "It was one of the last things we talked about before . . ." She waved her hand as if shooing something aside, pulled away from Rebekah, and stood up.

"How'd your mom die?" Rebekah asked, quietly.

"She had cancer. We knew it was coming, but I guess somehow I always made myself think she'd beat it, and then, when she didn't, I . . ."

"I'm sorry," Rebekah said, going to her again.

"I feel like such an idiot," Callie said. "I should be stronger."

Rebekah shook her head. "You have to give yourself time, Callie. You can't just expect to shove it all inside and be over it. That's not how you heal."

I stepped back toward the doorway, not sure what to do. I should have been the one who knew how to comfort Callie. I had lived through the death of a loved one. But her pain scared me, and Rebekah was doing a fine job, anyway.

I went back inside the house and busied myself rolling up sleeping bags.

When Mr. Cirone returned with an armful of small loaves of bread, *bolillos*, and the flatter *teleras*, which he said he'd purchased from a vendor who wouldn't say a word to him, not even *gracias*, we helped him try to convince people to eat. Except for Chad and Hope, and Judah, who declined even to get out of his sleeping bag to "rise and shine," everyone did.

At first, sitting in Dane Meyer's house doing nothing was a welcome reprieve after yesterday's grueling hike. But after three or four hours of it, several of us kids started pestering Mr. Cirone to let us go explore. Though visibly reluctant, undoubtedly because of the strange behavior of the people in the village, he eventually relented and went with seven of us for a walk around the plaza.

This plaza was unique in that there wasn't a Catholic church on it. A few fruit and vegetable tables, a meat market, a stand with the familiar witchcraft items for sale, and the shop where Mr. Cirone had bought our breakfast—that was about it. A few people hung in groups around each stand, stopping all their conversation to stare at us until we looked back at them.

"Why are they acting like that?" I asked Mr. Cirone. "It makes me nervous."

He smiled. "Don't be nervous, Miss Cook. Many of these people have probably never even been out of this village, and the ones who have, probably haven't been any farther than where we were yesterday. We represent a whole different world to them. I guess we could be a little intimidating."

"But wouldn't Mr. Meyer have told them we were coming?"

He nodded. "I would think so, anyway."

"They shouldn't be scared of us, then."

"I didn't say they were scared," he said. "Just keeping their distance until the common denominator gets into the picture."

"Mr. Meyer?"

"Mr. Meyer."

"That's another thing that's making me nervous," I admitted as I stepped slightly closer to him so that the others wouldn't hear me. "Where is he?"

Mr. Cirone chuckled. "You *are* nervous, aren't you?"

"Well?"

"It's a different life here, Ashton," he said. "Anything could have come up. A sickness. A birth. A death. A family receiving salvation. You never know on the mission field." He grinned. "The unpredictability is half the thrill."

"Thrill?" I smiled.

"Don't be afraid," Mr. Cirone urged. "We're going to be wise. I'm sure Dane will show up today or tomorrow. The people were willing to sell me bread this morning . . . by tonight, who knows? It can only get better as they get used to us being around. Everything will be all right. We'll just be a day or two behind schedule." He laughed. "You should be glad for the break. Building a church isn't easy work."

"I know." I supposed he was right. And, even if something was wrong, I wasn't going to remedy it by worrying about it. Especially since I didn't have a clue about what it might be. There was just that feeling along the back of my neck and that nagging in the back of my mind. *Something's wrong.*

Two times around the plaza satisfied us, and by lunch time, the noon heat had driven us back toward Mr. Meyer's house. While the others went ahead, Mr. Cirone and I stopped at the market to buy whatever was available for lunch—tortillas and boiled chicken—from the same old man who had sold us the bread that morning.

As his worn hands wrapped our tortillas in paper, he said, *"Buenos dias."*

I nodded and returned his greeting.

In Spanish, Mr. Cirone asked, "Where is Dane Meyer?"

The man acted as if he hadn't heard the question.

Mr. Cirone repeated it. *"¿Donde esta Dane Meyer, el mi-sionero?"* He turned and pointed past the door of the market at the pile of building materials across the plaza and at Mr. Meyer's house behind it. *"El que vive en esa casita."*

After straightening himself to his full height to look behind us, the man leaned toward us and whispered, *"Ix lichahuina kin puchinagan—"*

Mr. Cirone held up his hand—he clearly hadn't understood the old man's Totonaco, but two men entered the market behind us just then, and the vendor quickly turned toward them, away from us. We placed the money we owed him on the table and left.

Beside one of the buildings, several small children were play-ing with die-cast metal cars. *Where did they get those?* As soon as they saw us, they stood and ran. One of them, a little boy who couldn't have been older than three or four, tripped and fell to his knees in the dirt. He began to cry. One of the older children ran to him, but the little boy refused to budge from the spot.

"Go help him," Mr. Cirone urged me.

"Are you sure?"

"Yes. Go help him."

Shrugging—*If you say so*—I handed the package of tortillas to him and slowly, uncertainly, approached the wailing child. "Don't cry," I said softly as I knelt beside him. "It's okay . . . I mean, *es bueno.* Don't cry." The boys wouldn't understand the words, but maybe my tone would be soothing to them. "It's okay."

Gradually, the child settled down, and even let me help him to his feet and to wipe the dirt from his knees and palms. Only when the older boy smiled at me did I notice that all the other children who had been playing had gathered around me too. One of them spoke to me, and all the others laughed. I laughed with them, even though I had no idea what the girl had said. I barely understood Spanish, let alone the native language of these people.

But my laughter seemed to be the appropriate response. The little boy hugged me. Then slowly, one by one, the others stepped forward to do the same, stopping only when two women approached us and gently pulled them away from me.

I stood. "It's okay. *Es bueno.* Uh . . . *No problemo* . . . " Had I known at the beginning of my eighth-grade year that I'd someday find myself standing in the middle of the Mexican jungle, I might have given more thought to my "Nah" when Mom had asked me if I planned to sign up for Spanish.

We stared awkwardly at each other until one of the women smiled, pulled the boy who had fallen close to her, and nodded kindly at me.

I nodded back. What else could I do?

Still timid, but visibly less fearful, the women led the children away.

Mr. Cirone waited until they had left the plaza to join me. "I told you it could only get better."

I smiled. "I guess you were right."

Chapter 8

The tortillas, as always, were delicious, but I was unwilling to take my chances with anything else. Chicken had made me sick at home more than once. Here? I'd pass.

We ate the meal without conversation.

"Maybe we could start on the church," Shane suggested when he'd finished. "It's obvious where Mr. Meyer wants to put it."

"We might do that," said Mr. Cirone.

Silence.

"This house was not built for so many people," Todd complained.

Mr. Cirone smiled. "Feeling a bit cramped, are you?"

"And hot."

"I doubt that Dane had intended for all of us to stay here," Mrs. Cirone said.

Callie said, "I'm ready for a shower."

"Whenever I close my eyes," said Rebekah, "I see watermelon."

"Pizza."

"Iced tea . . ."

It didn't take long for this to irritate me. "We've only been in Mexico three days," I said. "Stop sniveling."

"She's right." Mrs. Cirone smiled. "Though some tact might have been appropriate."

Embarrassed, I looked down at my hands. "Sorry."

Mr. Cirone stood. "I think we need to be doing something. Let's get our gear together and hike on to the next village. Dane will either be there, or we'll meet him on the trail."

"What if he's not there?" Rebekah asked. "Or on the trail?"

I glanced quickly at Mr. Cirone. *See. I'm not the only one who's uneasy.*

"We'll cross that bridge if we get to it," he answered.

How can he be so undaunted?

"Listen," he said to all of us, "either God is in control, or He isn't. I happen to believe that He is." He grinned. "So let's get going."

God . . . in control. I didn't think I believed that anymore. How could I believe He'd been *in control* when Tommy had drowned? That would mean He'd had to sit back and allow it to happen. Watch it happen. In fact, wouldn't it mean He had *planned* it?

How could I accept that and still love Him?

I knew what the Bible said. About God working all things together for our good. About God's ways and understanding being far above ours. About the righteous being taken early to be spared from evil. That to be absent from the body is to be present with Christ. Yea, though I walk through the valley . . . I'd read the thoughts of men in too many sympathy cards. Good-bye is not forever in the Lord. Death is part of life. When you don't understand, find comfort in knowing He does. *God is in control.*

Once, I had believed that. But I realized, as I readied my pack for another day of hiking, that I had thrown that confidence away with the leftovers gone bad after Tommy's funeral.

Would I ever get it back?

After strapping my sleeping bag to the top of my pack, I sat down to retighten my boot laces. It promised to be another strenuous hike—only half as far as we'd come yesterday, but during the hottest part of the day.

"Sir?" Judah spoke to Mr. Cirone.

I glanced over at Judah. He'd been quiet, easy to overlook, all day, either asleep or sitting silently against the wall. He was still against the wall, sitting with his elbows on his knees and his face in his hands.

"Yes, what is it?" asked Mr. Cirone.

"Do we all have to go?" asked Judah quietly.

Mr. Cirone stopped loading his pack to look at him. "Are you still feeling sick?"

"No, sir. Maybe. I don't know." He glanced at me. "At the risk of adding to the sniveling . . . I just don't feel like hiking today."

"She apologized, Ewen," Chad said. "Leave it alone."

I looked quickly over at Mr. Marsh. This would be the second time he'd witnessed Chad's anger toward Judah. But, then . . . wasn't everyone a little grouchy this afternoon?

Mr. Marsh was looking steadily at Chad, but his expression revealed nothing.

"We don't all have to go," Mr. Cirone was saying. "I'm going to go, and I'll come back tonight. Anyone who wants to can come along."

Shane got quickly to his feet. "I'll go."

"Me too," I said.

Nobody else seized the opportunity.

"All right," Mr. Cirone said, after waiting several moments for some of the others to change their minds. None did. "I'll just bring a daypack, then, since it's only the three of us."

I didn't argue—the four miles in to the next village would be a lot easier without a pack. And I didn't ask *What if we don't find Mr. Meyer?* because I didn't want to do anything to make Mr. Cirone change his mind about leaving Mr. Meyer's house.

We headed toward the trail out of the village. Mr. Cirone. Me. Shane.

We walked. Half a mile in silence. Even without my pack, the steep terrain and Mr. Cirone's aggressive pace, combined with the heat of the afternoon, left me short-winded. But I did not complain or ask to rest.

One mile.

Two.

Shane kept right with me, helping me when we had to climb a boulder in the trail or duck under tangled ferns above it. The narrow dirt path seemed to be taking us right up the side of a mountain, but the denseness of the ferns and trees hid any view. We knew only that we'd walked about three miles when the trail let us out into a break in the jungle, and we stopped short.

I gasped.

"Oh no," Shane whispered.

In front of us, the sky reached down into a narrow but deep chasm. So deep that I could see the tops of trees several feet below me, and the mist and blue of water below them.

And where the trail met the edge of the chasm—a bridge. Ropes and planks of wood.

Nobody spoke for several minutes.

"I suppose the only other way across is ten miles away?" I asked, finally, forcing a smile.

"I don't know," Mr. Cirone admitted. "Dane and I didn't talk very much about this part of the area. He was going to be with us."

"Well . . . I'm sure it's the only way across. Otherwise, why would anyone use it?" I folded my arms across my chest and tried to ignore the fear tightening my shoulders as I imagined what it would feel like to actually walk on the thing. Two ropes, tied on this side around tree trunks that could have been a lot thicker, stretched through holes on both ends of thick but narrow planks of wood, spaced fairly evenly about six inches apart. Two more ropes were tied higher on the tree trunk and provided, for what it was worth, something to hold on to as you walked across the bridge.

"I think we'd better go one at a time," Mr. Cirone said. Then he looked over his shoulder at us. "Are both of you okay with this? We can go back and wait—"

I smiled even though my stomach felt like someone was kneading it. "I'm fine with it."

Shane only nodded.

"Okay." Mr. Cirone took in a deep breath. "I'll go first."

Shane and I stood at the edge and watched as Mr. Cirone crossed the bridge. He walked at a steady pace, keeping his eyes on the planks of wood at his feet, never looking, I noticed, off to either side.

I'd have to remember that when I went across.

I counted his steps, two hundred and six, and only let out my breath—I hadn't even realized I was holding it—when he stepped onto solid ground again on the other side of the chasm. Then I glanced at Shane. "My turn."

He nodded.

Grabbing the ropes in my hands, I licked my lips and stepped onto the first plank of wood. I tried to maintain as steady a pace as Mr. Cirone had, but the rocking of the bridge in the air unnerved me.

"Don't stop!" Mr. Cirone yelled to me. "Keep moving."

I obeyed him.

I did not have to look down to feel the huge emptiness there.

Concentrate on the next plank of wood.

That's what I did. Each plank shifted a little differently in response to my weight on it, but all of them held. I had never been so glad for the feel of earth beneath my feet as I was when I took Mr. Cirone's outstretched hand and joined him at the end of the bridge.

We both looked across to Shane.

He didn't move.

Mr. Cirone waved at him to go.

Still, he didn't move.

"He's scared," I said.

Mr. Cirone nodded. "So was I."

"Me, too," I admitted, since he had.

"One step at a time, Shane," Mr. Cirone encouraged. "You'll be fine."

Shane started across the bridge. His face was as blank and white as the mist at the bottom of the chasm, but he was moving.

"You're doing great," Mr. Cirone said. "Keep moving."

Shane kept walking. One step at a time, until he came to the middle of the bridge, where he turned his head only slightly to the right.

He stopped.

"Keep going, Shane!"

Shane pulled his attention away from the beautiful but terrifying vastness beside him and faced us again. His expression was no longer blank. It was an expression I'd seen only once before, but I'd never forgotten it.

I'd been fourteen. Hunting with Tommy and my father. We'd spent all morning tracking a moose in the low forest where much of the ground was marshy. My father had spotted a moose calf alone in the grass of a small clearing.

"Do you see the cow?" my father had asked us. No. Neither of us could see her. "Stay here," he said to me. He looked at Tommy. "You go around those trees and come in from behind her." Then he walked alone toward the clearing.

This was my first time hunting, and I wasn't sure I was going to like it. I had a rifle, and I knew how to use it. Politically correct or not, hunting had been a way of life in my father's family since his grandfather had settled in Alaska. Still . . . I knew that seeing the moose alive—so majestic and strong, not entirely beautiful, but . . . *alive*. And then . . .

I had waited on the edge of the clearing and watched my father.

Suddenly, there was a noise in the trees in the direction that Tommy had gone. A *crack* of branches. *Thudding* that I could feel in the earth beneath my feet. I raised my rifle.

I could see my brother's face, almost in slow motion, as he turned to see the animal charging through the trees. Toward him. Then I saw her. Steam came forcefully from her nostrils. She was huge. Her head. Her body. Her hooves.

I shouted, "Tommy!"

But he had frozen, his gun lifted but useless.

The moose would trample him without a second thought. *Never put yourself between a moose and her calf.*

"*Dad!*" But I knew he'd never get back to us in time.

In that brief but paralyzed instant, Tommy dropped his gun and ran.

"*Dad! Tommy!*"

He would never be able to outrun a charging moose!

The tall, dry mountain plants crunched flat as the moose thrust through them toward my brother.

I aimed my gun and fired.

"He's going to run," I whispered to Mr. Cirone, yanking myself back to the bridge. *Just like Tommy.* "He's going to run!"

And before the words were fully out of my mouth, Shane did exactly that.

Letting go of the ropes in his hands, and with his eyes wildly focused on the trees behind me, he ran.

"No!" Mr. Cirone shouted. "Shane! *STOP!*"

But Shane didn't stop.

Until one of his feet missed one of the planks of wood.

I screamed.

He fell. Full out, face first, onto the bridge. And somehow, it held him, even as it swung, wildly at first, and then more slowly back and forth. Left. Right. Left. Right. The ropes creaked eerily.

"Don't move," Mr. Cirone said calmly to Shane. "Just . . . don't . . . move."

Shane obeyed.

When the bridge finally stopped swinging, Mr. Cirone moved toward it.

"I'll go," I offered. "I'm lighter."

Reluctantly, but unable to dispute the wisdom of adding the least amount of weight to Shane's on the bridge, he nodded.

One plank at a time, with a firm hold on the ropes, I approached Shane. "It's all right," I kept telling him, though I could feel some strain in the ropes. "It's all right."

He lay perfectly still.

When I stood only inches away from him, I said, "Shane, get to your hands and knees slowly."

"I can't."

"You have to!" I held out my hand. "Here's my hand. I'll help you."

"I . . . can't."

More gently this time, I said, "You have to, Shane. And you can. Just . . . *try.*"

The next twenty seconds, as Shane worked his way to his feet, seemed to take as long to pass as my entire high school career. But I let him take the time he needed.

Placing Shane's left hand over the rope, and my hand over his, I led him to the end of the bridge, to solid ground, where he sat down heavily and lowered his head to his knees.

I sat quietly beside him with one hand on his shoulder just as I had done for my brother that day at the marsh. Like Tommy, he needed several moments to stop trembling, and then he spent several more apologizing.

I'd not gone hunting again after that trip, but this time, there would be no such weakness. Sooner or later we would have to cross the bridge again to get back over to the other side of the chasm. Would Shane be able to handle it?

He'd have to. That's all. He'd have to.

"Are you hurt?" Mr. Cirone asked him.

"No, sir."

Just his ego, I thought. *Just like Tommy.* But he needn't be ashamed, and I told him so.

He thanked me for saying it, but he clearly didn't believe it.

We started walking again, leaving the bridge behind us.

"Ashton?"

I glanced over my shoulder at Shane.

"Thanks," he said. "For helping me."

"You'd have done it for me, right?" I grinned. He'd already proved that by going after the boy who'd stolen my sack.

He nodded. "Still . . . thanks."

For forty-five minutes or more, we pressed silently along the path. The air hung so thick and heavy with moisture, and so still, that it felt as if we were carving our way through it. I wondered what had inspired the original builders of these villages to settle here. Had they escaped to avoid the conquistadors? Or had they been fleeing wars among themselves? Perhaps they'd come here to enjoy the abundant food supply or for some religious reason. Or maybe I was painting too much into the picture . . . everybody has to live somewhere. *Here* was as good a place as any, right?

And yet . . . the idea of God's love for every individual seemed somehow more tangible to me here in the deep jungle. The people living here might live out their entire lives forgotten by the rest of the world, but not one of them had been overlooked by God. The proof was that He had taken the time to inspire Dane Meyer, and many others like him, to forfeit their comfortable lives back home to bring the gospel to them. "*How can they hear without a preacher?*"

The people here had a preacher, all right. If only we could find him!

"Are there more villages beyond the one we're going to?" I asked Mr. Cirone.

"Yes."

"So . . . can we expect a longer hike if Mr. Meyer isn't there?"

Mr. Cirone shook his head. "We'll go back tonight, one way or the other. My first responsibility is to you kids."

"But you'll be worried, then, won't you," Shane asked, "about Mr. Meyer?"

"I'll be curious," Mr. Cirone conceded.

Chapter 9

Mr. Cirone stopped so suddenly in front of me that I nearly ran into him.

"Shhh," he whispered. "I heard something."

I almost laughed. We were in the middle of the jungle, and he was alarmed because he heard something? But a sudden dryness in my mouth kept me quiet. What could he have heard? Something unusual, obviously, but how had he heard it above the racket of insects, birds, and water all around us?

He didn't tell us. He just stood still for several moments, listening, and then signaled to us when he was ready to start moving again.

I followed him quietly, grateful that Shane was behind me. My eyes and ears were suddenly alert and my nerves on edge. The afternoon, already stressful, had turned frightening, as well.

"What was it?" Shane asked after a while.

"Probably nothing," Mr. Cirone replied. "I thought I heard voices."

"People?"

He nodded.

"I didn't see anyone," I said.

"Neither did I. That's the point."

Clearly, I had missed something.

Mr. Cirone explained. "It wouldn't be unusual to run into someone on this trail, so when I heard voices, I didn't think anything of it . . . until we didn't see anyone."

"Hmm," Shane said, behind me. "Maybe we scared them and they hid from us."

"Maybe." Mr. Cirone nodded. "Maybe."

I laughed nervously. "What else could it be?"

"The followers of some demonic pagan god looking for their next sacrifice," Shane crooned as he lunged forward and grabbed me from behind.

I screamed and then laughed as I spun around to face him. "Loser! Don't do that!"

Mr. Cirone did not appreciate our amusement. "Stay quiet," he whispered. His authority earned our obedience. His intensity kept it.

We walked.

"Shouldn't we be there by now?" I whispered. I was beginning to feel tired and had to go to the bathroom.

"I thought it was four miles in," Mr. Cirone said, "but we've walked that far already."

"At least," agreed Shane.

"Maybe you were wrong about how far it was," I suggested.

"Must have been." Mr. Cirone pulled off his daypack and sat on a rock beside the trail. "We'll rest here and then head back. We want to be sure we still have light to get back across that bridge."

"Maybe it would be better in the dark," Shane muttered as he sat beside Mr. Cirone.

"Trust me when I tell you it wouldn't be." Mr. Cirone's eyes stayed serious even as he grinned.

"I'd love to stick around and hear about how you know this, Mr. Cirone," I said, "but I really need to find a private place."

He nodded. "Just don't go too far."

"I won't. Don't worry." I stepped off the trail into the jungle and started making my way down a hill toward a thick snarl of trees. This was the one aspect of adventure in the great outdoors that I had always hated—the pristine bathroom facilities.

On the trail behind me, Shane and Mr. Cirone talked quietly. I could hear their voices through the trees—first Shane's, then Mr. Cirone's, then Shane's again—but I couldn't make out their words.

I stepped around and behind a stand of three huge trees.

Private? Definitely. Because of the thick leaves above me that seemed to reach to the sky, the place was dark and pleasantly cool. I listened, but could no longer hear Shane and Mr. Cirone.

Safe.

I started to loosen my belt.

But I heard something behind me. Something too big to be a bird or a spider. And then, before I could turn around and see what it was . . . before I could even scream, it grabbed me, covered my mouth, and held me so tightly that I thought my arms would break.

I struggled uselessly.

A man! It was a man! What would a man be doing *here?*

"I'm going to let you go," he whispered in my ear. *English! He's speaking English!* "Don't scream! Please don't scream."

I nodded, suddenly as curious as I was terrified.

He released me and then quickly turned me to face him.

Though I'd fully intended to scream, all I could do was stand there and stare.

Mr. Meyer!

"I know you . . . don't I?" He stepped back, lowered himself stiffly to the ground, and leaned back against one of the trees.

"A-Ashton Cook, sir." I knelt on the ground beside him.

"Ashton . . ." His face was bruised and dirty. He looked pale and exhausted. And he was clutching his left side as if it hurt.

"Mr. Meyer, what—?"

"Ashton Cook. I remember you. You were just a kid when I left. I'm sorry I scared you, . . . but I had to make sure you didn't scream. That would have been too dangerous."

"It's okay," I said. "Too dangerous? Why? What—?"

"There isn't time to explain," he said, shaking his head. "They're out there. Looking for me."

"Who? Mr. Meyer, what—?"

He leaned toward me, grabbed my shoulders in his hands, and stared intently, almost pleadingly, at me. "Listen, you just have to trust me and do exactly as I say. If you don't, I won't be safe, and you and the others might not be either."

I was listening.

"Go back to my house as if you never saw me. Don't tell any-one you saw me until you're safely there. Some of these people know English, and if they hear you . . . " He squinted and shook his head. "You don't even want to think about that. Just go back to my house, build the church, just like you're still waiting for me. Stay in the village. You'll be safe there."

"Some of *what* people?" I asked, confused. "What about you? Why don't you come back with us? What . . . ?"

"It's enough for you to know that there are some people who don't want me around anymore. Read my journal when you get to my house. That'll answer some of your questions. I'm going to go for help. If these people find me, they'll probably kill me. If they think you've seen me . . . you just can't let that happen. You'll be safe in the village. It might take me a couple days to get past them . . . I'll have to find another way across . . . they'll be watching the bridge." He'd said that last sentence more to himself than to me. "Go, now, in case anyone was watching you."

"I . . . I don't understand."

"I know you don't." He stood and held his hand out to me. When I took it, he said, "I'll be all right, and so will you, as long as you do what I said. Build the church. I'll be back before you finish."

I didn't know what he was talking about, so how could I argue? Why couldn't Mr. Cirone have run into him instead of me? He'd have known what to do. I trusted Mr. Meyer . . . and, more than that, the look in his eyes made me afraid to do anything but obey him . . . but . . . *what if he never comes back?*

"Go!" he whispered.

I did. It took all of my will to walk back up the hill to Shane and Mr. Cirone without glancing over my shoulder. To act as if nothing much had happened in that stand of trees. As I rejoined the others, I adjusted my belt a bit in case anyone might be watching me.

I could wait to go to the bathroom, but could I walk all the way back to the village without revealing my secret? I'd have to . . . that was all. Just like Shane would have to get across that bridge. I'd have to keep my mouth shut.

"Got any more of those?" I asked Mr. Cirone when I sat beside him on the trail again, pointing at the granola bar he was eating.

He tossed one to me, and I ate it. It tasted like mud and raisins.

We sat in the shade for nearly half an hour and then started back toward the chasm. The bridge. Mr. Meyer's house. And, I hoped, answers.

I forced myself to breathe slowly and laugh at Mr. Cirone's occasional attempts at humor even though I felt as if every muscle in my body was trying to tighten in around my lungs. I couldn't get enough air. The late afternoon heat wasn't helping either. All I could think about was Mr. Meyer running through the jungle, hiding from I didn't know who, trying to go for help and not get killed in the process. And that we'd have to spend the next few days building a church as if our only concern was the effects of the sun and so much sweating on our young and unpredictable complexions.

And, of course, Shane, Mr. Cirone, and I still had to get across that stupid bridge.

Was I expected to look at all these terrifying and seemingly misplaced pictures around me and paste them all together somehow into a *Don't worry, God is in control* collage that I could find strength in? I could barely scrape together enough confidence in God to trust Him to work out even *one* of these situations. All of them? At the same time?

I could only pray that He'd prove my lack of trust as being sinful and wrong.

"How much farther to the bridge?" Shane asked.

"Half a mile, or so," Mr. Cirone answered.

"Is it my imagination, or is it starting to get dark already?"

I looked up through the trees. "It's your imagination."

Nobody suggested it, but we all began to walk faster.

When we arrived at the edge of the bridge twenty minutes later and Mr. Cirone had gotten safely to the other side, I gently squeezed Shane's arm and asked, "Do you want me to go across with you?"

"It's more dangerous that way," he said, swallowing hard. "I . . . I asked God to go with me."

Such a childlike thing to say! And yet, I could see in Shane's eyes how much he meant it, and though he might be a little embarrassed about admitting it, he was not ashamed of having done it.

"He will." I let go of his arm.

Shane stepped onto the bridge. It swayed slowly with each step he took, but he did not turn his head. One step after the other, he walked until his left foot, and then his right, came down on solid ground, and he turned to wave me forward.

For some reason, going back across was easier. Maybe because I had already done it once. Or maybe it was something more.

Neither Mr. Cirone nor I made a big deal about congratulating Shane.

We just thanked God.

Chapter 10

The sun had nearly set by the time Mr. Cirone pulled open the door to Mr. Meyer's house. Quietly, the three of us stepped inside. Nearly everyone was lying on his sleeping bag already, turning in for the night. But nobody was asleep.

Mrs. Cirone stood to greet her husband. "You didn't find Dane."

"No."

"Yes," I said, "we did."

In the stunned silence, I reported my encounter with Mr. Meyer and repeated his words as accurately as I could. When I finished, I said, "I wanted to tell you right away, Mr. Cirone."

"I'm sure you did."

"Should I have?"

He thought for a long moment. "I don't know, Miss Cook. You weren't wrong not to, considering what he told you. I just wish I had talked to him."

"His journal!" I blurted, surprised because I'd nearly forgotten to mention it. "He said we'd get the answers we needed in his journal!"

"I'll look for it," volunteered Mrs. Cirone. As soon as she found it—in Mr. Meyer's bottom drawer underneath his shirts—she handed it to her husband, who sat down in a corner with his flashlight and began to read it.

Silently.

"He'll tell us all the relevant stuff in the morning," Mrs. Cirone whispered to Shane, me, and the rest of the kids. "We should try to get some sleep. It might be a long next few days."

Slowly, while the house quieted and nearly everyone lay down again and tried to pretend that the darkness was cooler than the day had been, I crossed the room and stepped outside. My muscles were tense, and my nerves were on edge. There was no way I was going to get to sleep any time soon. I sat on the wooden bench in front of the house and stared vacantly out across the plaza.

After a while Rebekah came outside, too, and sat beside me.

"How's Callie doing?" I asked her.

"All right," she said. "Mrs. Cirone has been spending lots of time with her. Can I ask you something, Ashton?"

"Sure."

"Why didn't you come over and talk to her this morning? I mean, you've been there. I felt really at a loss to know what to say."

"You did fine," I told her.

"I don't know," she said. "How did you handle it . . . when Tommy died? The closest I've ever come to losing someone I cared about was . . ." A look like that of someone catching herself just as she was about to blab about a surprise party to the birthday girl flashed across Rebekah's face, and she shut her mouth. "I just can't even imagine living with that kind of pain."

"It's hard," I said. "Hard doesn't even begin to describe it. But, you know, you have to move on. You just say, 'Okay, God, I don't understand this, but, for whatever reason, it was okay with You, so . . .'" I shrugged. "You have to accept it and move on."

She shook her head. "There's no way it's that easy."

I stood up. "What are you going to do? Go around blubbering all the time? Being angry all the time? Thinking 'if only' all the time? Hating the person who—" Now I shut my mouth. "You know what, Rebekah? I'm thinking you and I might not want to be talking about this."

"I'm sorry. I shouldn't have brought it up," she said. "You're right."

I sat beside her again.

How had I "handled" Tommy's death? I'd cried . . . a little. I'd gotten angry . . . a little. But while most people would whine about their offenses or the seven hundred and sixty-two things that annoyed them most about life, I'd always been happy to shove it inside and try to forget about it. Well, maybe happy wasn't exactly the right word. Maybe I just felt that that was my only truly safe option. And that's exactly what I'd done after Tommy's death. I didn't let myself think about him. It was that simple. I didn't allow myself to think about Judah, or how I felt about what had happened at the river.

And I realized now, as I sat beside Rebekah, that I hadn't allowed myself to think about God either. I didn't go to Him for comfort. I didn't blame Him. I didn't ask Him why.

I'd just . . . moved on.

How had I "handled" Tommy's death? I recalled what Chad had said. *That's your trick, isn't it? 'If I don't think about it, it'll be okay.'* And I recalled what Rebekah had said to Callie earlier that morning. *You can't just expect to shove it all inside and be over it. That's not how you heal.*

I was beginning to think that maybe I hadn't "handled" Tommy's death at all.

Rebekah and I didn't talk anymore. She eventually surrendered to her tiredness and went inside. Still wide awake, I stayed outside to wait for morning. It seemed as though the sun would never rise. Long, long hours. But I fell asleep at some point and was awakened by the screen door being pulled open beside me. Mr. Cirone held the door for Mr. Marsh, Judah, and Chad, who'd apparently followed him to the house from the darkness of the jungle, and then went inside behind them.

None of them had looked particularly happy.

Mrs. Cirone joined me on the bench.

"I must have been doing some serious sleeping when you all left," I said nervously. "I can't believe I didn't hear you."

She smiled and nodded.

I wasn't surprised that the five of them had gone out for a little private conversation. The Cirones clearly weren't the type of youth leaders to tolerate unresolved tension, and Chad had been about as successful at hiding his as a three-year-old is when she's told to share the nice dolly with her sister.

"I'd been wondering," Mrs. Cirone said after a moment, "since the day we all met at the airport what was between you three. When none of you said anything to us, I passed it off as a misread, but—"

"It wasn't a misread," I said. "But I guess you know that now."

She nodded. "And now that I do, I hope you'll come talk to me if you want or need to."

"Thanks," I said.

"Would you tell me what happened, Ashton?"

"Why?" I squinted at her. "Isn't that what Chad and Judah just did?"

"Yes. But not everyone remembers everything the same way."

I sighed. "There's not too much to misremember, Mrs. Cirone. Judah and Tommy went camping. On the way home, Tommy wanted to take the shortcut across the river, but Judah didn't. Tommy said he was going to, no matter what. Judah let him. Tommy got in trouble on his horse in the river and drowned. That's it."

Her silence beside me unnerved me.

"You said that like someone listing the directions for making macaroni and cheese," she said, finally. Quietly.

The observation embarrassed me . . . because it was accurate. "I'm sorry," I said. "I don't mean to make it sound like I don't care about what happened. It's just that . . . well, it was a long time ago, and I've said it so many times, and I don't like to talk about it at all."

"I can understand that," Mrs. Cirone said. Then she said, "You don't seem to have the same anger about it that Chad does."

"I'd think you'd think that was a good thing."

"Do you blame Judah?" she asked.

I stared up at the sunless—and now moonless—sky. Black. "I don't know. I mean, I guess so. If Judah had gone with Tommy, it could have changed the way it turned out. But, you know, I don't dwell on it. It's healthier not to dwell on it."

"That depends," she said, "on whether you're not dwelling on it because you've forgiven, or if you're just . . . hiding from it."

"How can I hide from it, Mrs. Cirone? My brother's dead. I don't see him at breakfast anymore. We don't fight anymore. His room is empty. We don't play basketball out in the driveway any—" I shook my head. "I just don't dwell on it."

Mrs. Cirone let it go, and I was glad.

In its time, the sun did rise. Mrs. Cirone and I watched together as it turned the sky from black to gray-blue . . . which was the color it stayed, and dense clouds began to let loose their moisture in huge, surprisingly warm drops.

We hurried inside.

The noise of the rain on the roof, soft at first, but growing louder and louder, eventually woke everyone, and we gathered in a circle to pray together for Mr. Meyer's safety.

Because of the rain, there was nothing else to do when we finished but return to our sleeping bags. And that's what almost everyone did.

But Judah sat beside me. "Do you remember when Mr. Meyer took our fifth- and sixth-grade classes on that backpacking trip?"

"Yeah."

"He's good in rough country, Ash," he said. "I'm sure he'll be okay."

"There are men out there who want to kill him," I reminded him.

"I know," he said. "We've got to believe that God will protect him."

"Like He protected Tommy?" Even before I finished the sentence, I regretted having started it. "I'm sorry, Judah. This isn't about Tommy. It just . . . came out." And where had it come from? I'd never even allowed myself to *think* something like that, let alone *say* it. Not even in the days following Tommy's drowning, when so many of the people around me were questioning God and blaming Judah and telling me it was okay to be angry.

Judah nodded as he stood up. He opened his mouth to say something, but apparently thought better of it. Turning away, he walked across the room, back to his sleeping bag.

Someone else took his place beside me. Mrs. Cirone.

She said, "Ashton, do you know the Scripture in Isaiah about the bruised reed and the smoldering wick?"

I had to smile. "Not right offhand. But give me time. I'm sure it'll come to me."

She laughed, but only for a second.

"Why?" I asked her.

"It says that God won't break a bruised reed or snuff out a barely burning candle."

"Uh-huh," I said, more than a little confused. Why was she quoting Scripture to me?

She admitted, "I overheard you and Judah just now."

I waited. What was she trying to say? "And that Scripture had *what* to do with what Judah was saying?"

But someone called her over to the table, and she stood and walked away without answering. Apparently, I was expected to figure it out for myself.

It rained.

The slightly cooler temperature that began as a blessing soon became an irritation because walls made of sticks tied together with vines and an aging thatched roof do not make for an entirely waterproof house. Besides the water dripping in on us through various cracks in the walls and ceiling, fingers of water poked their way inside through places in the foundation where the mud had begun to pull away from the stone, turning the edges of the dirt floor muddy. The one good thing was that we were able to gather several gallons of clean, pure, drinking water.

I thought frequently about Mr. Meyer, out there in the jungle, and prayed that he'd stay safe.

For the first time since arriving in Mexico, I slid *inside* my sleeping bag. Even there, though, I couldn't escape the dampness in the air. And even though I was exhausted because I hadn't slept for a long time, I forced myself to stay awake. Mr. Cirone had gone to get us breakfast, and I wanted to be up when he returned . . . not because I was hungry, but because I knew he'd tell us about Mr. Meyer's journal then, and I did not want to miss a word of it.

An hour passed before he arrived back, soaked and empty-handed.

He took the dry clothes his wife held out to him and stepped behind the curtained-off corner of the house to change into them. When he came out into the main room again, he apologized to us. "I guess we'll have to do without the most important meal of the day today."

Nobody complained.

He grabbed Mr. Meyer's one chair, placed it in a spot where water wouldn't drip on him, and sat down. "I need you all to listen to me for a few minutes."

Everyone was already listening.

"When Dane got here five years ago," he began, "he met up with the usual resistance to the gospel—idol worship, witchcraft, apathy, the people's fear of him—the first white man some of them had seen. He built his house. Tried to adapt to the ways of the village. Eventually doors began to open for him to share the gospel, first with one man, then his family, then another, and another, until about half the village had accepted Christ. This took about three years. Dane thought everything was going well . . . until he found out what many of his new converts did to earn their living." He paused.

We waited.

"There are two main industries around here," he said simply. "Coffee and drugs. Deeper into this jungle than Dane had ever gone, there is a huge drug operation. Many of the people in all these little villages along the trail do some job or another for the *narcotraficantes*—drug traffickers. Some of them do the actual harvesting. Some of them manufacture the drugs into a salable form. Others transport them. This pretty much goes unopposed by local police and other authorities, Dane found out the hard way, because the drug traffickers have paid them off. This is big money. Big."

I sat up. My sleeping bag slipped off my shoulders. I didn't move to pull it back up.

"Most of the people Dane talked with didn't know what they were producing. They'd been told lies—this is used for cooking, or for medicine, or to treat animals with worms. They had no idea that they were part of something as illegal and harmful as drug trafficking. So, when Dane told them the truth, it caused a big dilemma for them. How could they serve this new God they'd embraced and still be part of what they were doing? And yet, it was their livelihood. When several of them decided to quit, then they found out that angering the people they worked for could be a dangerous thing. Some of their houses were burned. People were physically assaulted, including Dane. Some caved in and went back to work, but many didn't.

For about a year, these villages struggled with this, but it seemed to have let up in the past year or so. That's when Dane decided he'd build a church here. The people had made a strong stand for Christ. They wanted him to stay. There hadn't been any trouble for a long time. When I wrote to him about the possibility of bringing a team to help him, he mentioned the drug situation briefly, but he thought it wouldn't be a problem."

Mr. Cirone chuckled bitterly. "I didn't think twice about it. We've taken teams all over Central and South America. If we refused to take the gospel anywhere where people were growing illegal drugs, we'd be denying a whole lot of people the most important opportunity of their lives."

"That's for sure," agreed Mrs. Cirone.

"Other than making arrangements for our arrival," Mr. Cirone continued, "Dane's last journal entries seemed routine enough. A couple of births. A death from an insect bite. Being called to a village fifteen miles away to pray with an old man who wanted to receive Christ . . ." He thought for a moment. "That was three days before we were due to arrive."

"I wonder if he ever made it there," Mrs. Cirone said. "Or if that old man really exists."

"What would make the drug people decide to harass him now, after they'd left him alone for so long?" I asked.

"Good question." Mrs. Cirone looked to her husband.

"That I couldn't tell you. Maybe they felt threatened by the idea of his building the church. Maybe they saw his trip alone into the jungle as their chance to see him 'accidentally' disappear, never to get in their way again. I don't know." He stood to his feet as if he couldn't stay still. "The thing is, they did move against him, and he's clearly in a lot of danger."

"Can we help him?" Shane asked.

"That's what we have to talk about next." Mr. Cirone sat again, leaned forward with his elbows on his knees, and rested his chin on his clasped hands. "From what Dane said to Ashton, he seems to think we'd be safe to stay here and build the church. I tend to agree. One man disappearing in the jungle isn't far-fetched at all. Thirteen of us . . . that would be too risky for them. If we all bolted, they might suspect that we know what's going on, though, and could decide it's worth the risk. I can see Dane's reasoning. And yet . . . my first responsibility is for your safety. Would your parents want me keeping you here when there's a known danger like the one we seem to have gotten ourselves into the middle of?" He glanced around the room at each one of us. "Do *you* want to stay here, knowing all this?"

"I do," Shane said.

Hope, Callie, Judah, Rebekah, and I all said the same.

Mr. Cirone looked at the rest of the team. They were in, they said.

"Okay," said Mr. Cirone. "If anyone wants to go back, Mr. Marsh will take you. I don't think a few of you going would raise any questions or suspicion." He paused. "And there's no need to feel ashamed if that's what you decide."

"I'm staying," Shane said. "No question."

The rest of us nodded our *Me too's*.

"Well," said Mr. Cirone, standing again, "when it stops raining, we'll go see what we can do about getting to work on building ourselves a church. There are going to have to be rules. Nobody leaves sight of this house. Nobody talks about Dane Meyer. As far as anyone who might overhear us is concerned, we're still waiting for him to show up."

"One thing, Mr. Cirone," Rebekah said.

"Go ahead."

"If the drug guys are against the idea of Mr. Meyer putting up his church, they might not just sit by and let us do it."

"Good point. If there's any sign of hostility toward us, we'll reevaluate." He looked from person to person again. "Okay?"

One by one, we nodded.

"It might take Dane several days to get out of the jungle," Mr. Cirone said, "and several more to find and bring back help. He'll probably have to get all the way back to Poza Rica to find an authority he can be sure hasn't been paid off by these drug guys.

Every step of the way will be dangerous for him. I'd say more than anything else we can do, he needs us to pray for him."

"I just wish we could know where he is," Rebekah said, "and if he's all right."

Mr. Cirone nodded. "So do I. But we can't. All we can do is find strength in the fact that God knows."

Even if God does know, that doesn't guarantee He'll protect him! God certainly knew where Tommy was, and he's dead.

My thoughts must have shown in my face because Mr. Cirone looked right at me and said, "Sometimes things happen that we can't understand. Things that we are sure cannot be part of God's will. And yet they happen. Then we question God, and we even get angry at Him. This is one of those times.

"Why would God let something bad happen to someone who's given the past five years of his life to sharing the gospel with people here? How many missionaries have died in the past two thousand years? How many have been beaten? How many have had their entire family killed right in front of them by someone trying to make them deny Christ? And not just missionaries either. Christians all over the world suffer.

"But we always have to keep in mind that Time is like a multibillion piece puzzle to God. He knows how it all goes together, and He's putting it together, piece by piece. He knows what the finished product is going to look like. He designed it! When our pieces go in, they may not make sense to us. 'What's this blue corner for? Why is this yellow piece down here? What could be the good in this spot of green?' "

Mr. Cirone smiled. "But God knows. It's not even really a puzzle to Him. He's just laying the pieces in. Carefully. In the order He's arranged. And when He puts that last piece in, all those unexplained blue corners and spots of green will make sense. We'll see their part in the whole picture. And it'll be beautiful." He laughed. "And you thought you weren't going to have to listen to any silly sermon illustrations for three weeks!"

"It wasn't silly," Callie said.

Simplistic, maybe, I thought, but definitely not silly. "That doesn't leave much room for our free will," I said. There was nothing else to do. Why not debate some doctrine? Pastor Ewen always said that you could learn a lot about a person from the way he or she debated doctrine.

"I look at it this way," Mr. Cirone said, sitting down again, "we don't surprise God with any act of our free will. We can grieve Him. We can please Him. But we don't surprise Him, either way. He doesn't sit up in heaven and say, 'Oh no! Oh, Angels, what am I going to do? Ashton down there in Alaska did such and such, and now my whole plan for eternity is going to have to be rewritten!' "

Everyone laughed. Even me. The picture was absurd.

"Point taken," I said, serious again. "But there are things, some really hard things, that don't make sense."

Mr. Cirone nodded. "I know. But see, Ashton, even if you can't see our lives as part of the whole picture that God is creating . . . then let's suppose everything is random. Keep in mind, though, that the Bible does say we'll reap what we sow. It does say we choose to serve God or not. We even choose *how* we serve God. Okay, so, where does that leave us? Where does that leave God? Instead of saying He's doing a puzzle, let's say, like it does in Isaiah and Jeremiah, that He's a potter, working with clay. Have you ever worked with clay on a potter's wheel?"

I shook my head.

"It's harder than it looks," he said. "A potter has a picture in his mind of what he wants this lump of clay to look like and be used for when he's finished. But clay does its own thing sometimes. The potter has to keep at it. Molding it in his hands. Adding water to it at just the right times. Keeping the wheel spinning at a steady pace." He smiled and laughed a little. "Thank God, He doesn't have the temper of some artists I've seen who get frustrated, yank their lump of clay off the wheel, and throw it to the floor."

"A bruised reed shall He not break."

I glanced over at Mrs. Cirone. *Me. She'd been talking about me.*

"Eventually, Ashton," Mr. Cirone said, "and always, He finishes the pot."

"Something else," Mrs. Cirone said, looking at no one in particular, "you've got a promise that God will work all things—even those difficult things we can't understand—for good."

Since it was still early morning, I lay back down then and pulled my sleeping bag over my head. More than the rain pelting on the roof or the wetness of the air or the tense waiting and concern for Mr. Meyer—more than any of that, I tried to ignore the clamor inside my own head.

But I could not ignore it.

. . . a puzzle . . . The Potter . . . clay does its own thing sometimes . . . a multibillion piece puzzle . . . You were just a kid when I left . . . That's not how you heal . . . or if you're just hiding . . . a bruised reed . . . Me. She was talking about me.

And it'll be beautiful.

I realized, as I lay there, that I wanted to believe that. But I hadn't been. I wanted to believe that God could take something as horrible and pointless and painful as my brother's death and somehow work good from it. But I didn't know how.

I don't know how!

A bruised reed. Mrs. Cirone had gotten it exactly right.

Chapter 11

By lunch time the rain had stopped, and the jungle smelled wet and alive and new. It didn't take long, though, for the heat of the afternoon sun to completely supplant the cool of the morning. In fact, it seemed hotter because of the extra moisture lingering in the air. Mr. Cirone was able to purchase some tortillas from the man who'd sold us bread the day before, and we ate them gratefully. And somewhat ravenously.

"I'm still hungry," Shane said when all the tortillas were gone. "Can I go buy more?"

Mr. Cirone nodded and handed him some money. "Take someone with you."

I volunteered.

Shane and I walked quickly toward the market. It was difficult to behave casually, as though I didn't know that there might be people watching me. Every movement in the trees beside or behind us tempted me to turn my head. And there was so much more movement in the trees than I'd ever noticed before that I knew it had to be a trick of the situation. So I kept my eyes directed straight ahead.

"Did you get any sleep this morning?" Shane asked me.

"A little."

A man carrying a basket of fruit hurried past us with his head down.

I wondered if these people knew about what had happened to Mr. Meyer. Maybe they'd been in on it. Or maybe they knew nothing but only suspected. All of these possibilities could explain why they seemed to be working so hard to avoid and ignore us.

Fear.

Something I'd certainly tasted recently . . . more than I'd bargained for.

I stepped closer to Shane.

We entered the shade of the market and bought our tortillas. Because the old man was busy again with other customers, we didn't attempt any communication with him except to thank him. As we stepped back out onto the plaza, someone grabbed my arm. I wanted to scream, but held my reaction to a gasp.

"What?" Shane tensed beside me.

I turned away from him to see who had grabbed me.

The little boy who had fallen in the plaza yesterday! I smiled, let out my breath, got down on my knee, and waited to see what he wanted. When he held out a small cross made of two sticks tied together with red string, I nodded. "Jesus."

"Jesus," the boy repeated, obviously struggling to pronounce it as I had. He held the cross out closer to me. "*Puchina.*"

Puchina. Was this a Spanish word or Totonaco? What did it mean?

I glanced at Shane, not sure what the little boy wanted.

"I think he's trying to give it to you," Shane said.

Looking questioningly back at the boy, I touched my chest with my forefinger.

His smile broadened into something so innocent and absolute that I would have hugged him except that it might make some of the adults standing nearby nervous. Instead, I said, "Thank you," and held my hand open in front of him.

He laid the cross gently on my palm, giggled a little, and then ran away from me.

Tightening my hand around the tiny cross, I stood. "How sweet."

"Yeah." Shane grinned. "He thinks you're cute."

"Be quiet!" I felt my face flush and looked away from Shane so that he wouldn't notice. "He fell down yesterday, and I helped him. That's all."

"Uh-huh. He thinks you're cute."

I ignored him this time, and we started walking back toward Mr. Meyer's house.

"Where do you suppose he got the cross?" Shane asked.

"Mr. Meyer, I'm sure."

"I wish we could get through to one of the adults who could actually talk to us the way you got through to that little boy."

I nodded. That would be helpful. But I doubted that any of the adults were going to fall in the dirt in the plaza and start crying for help any time soon. "We already know what we have to do," I said. "It would just be nice if we knew whether these people were with us or against us."

"Shh," Shane warned.

"Oh, yeah. Sorry."

Shane grinned. "I still say that little guy thought you were cute."

"Would you drop it?"

When we got back to Mr. Meyer's house, we handed out tortillas to the kids who were still hungry. After giving one to Rebekah, I held one out to Judah, who was sitting beside her. I'd noticed that he hadn't eaten any from the batch Mr. Cirone had brought. "Aren't you going to eat?"

"You should try," Mrs. Cirone said to him as she joined me. The two of us stood over him, and Rebekah watched him, waiting.

He laughed. "Looks like I'm not going to have much of a choice."

"You need to eat," Mrs. Cirone said. "I know you don't feel hungry, and I know you're afraid you'll eat it, only to see it again later . . . which you probably will . . . but you do need to eat."

Grimacing almost, Judah held his hand out for a tortilla. "One," he said. "I'll eat one."

I smiled and gave it to him. Then I showed him and Rebekah the cross the little boy had given me.

"I remember making things like that in children's church," he said.

"That's right. We did." I remembered. "When Mr. Meyer was our teacher."

"Mm hmm."

"I hope he's okay." I couldn't help looking at the jungle on the other side of the window.

Judah eventually finished his tortilla and half of a second one, and then Mrs. Cirone ordered him to lie down and get some rest. He complained that he was bored of sleeping, but Mrs. Cirone held fast to her policy of never allowing herself to be deterred by a "whiny" teenager.

"We'd never get anything done on these trips," she declared, "if we caved in and put something off every time a kid started to blubber and bellow about it." Though her attitude was one of kidding around, the concern behind it showed in her face.

When everyone had finished eating, Mr. Cirone stood and went to the door. "Come on," he said. "Let's go see what we can get done on the church."

Even though the heat pressed down upon and through us, nobody complained about working. In fact, being outside and doing something seemed to improve the overall mood. Some of us used brooms and rakes to smooth and level the dirt in the area that would be the church floor. Some used knives and machetes to remove the tufts of grassy leaves from the bamboo poles. Some dug holes for the main support poles around the perimeter of the building and for the two in the center that would stabilize the roof.

Some dug a narrow but fairly deep trench between the support poles where we'd begin to lay the foot-and-a-half high foundation. And some began assembling the roof structure, the *armazon*, with sticks and some of the larger bamboo poles cut down the middle.

Several people in the plaza stopped to watch us. Nobody stepped forward to help us, but they didn't try to stop us either. So we worked.

Three years earlier, our family had added a room onto our house in Alaska. We had done the work ourselves, so I thought I knew what I was getting into when I signed up for this trip. It seemed, at the time, that it could only be easier in Mexico. There would be no electrical wiring to figure out. No plumbing. But back home, all our logs had been precut and sized to fit exactly against each other. We'd had electric tools. A floor plan. And the temperature had been a lot more comfortable.

The Ewens had helped us. Tommy, Judah, Nathan, Rachel, and I had done the entire roof by ourselves. I remembered the day we finished. The five of us stood on the dock, looking up at our handiwork, then out over the lake at the mountain, and finally at one another. I remembered our shared sense of a difficult job well done.

I squinted my eyes shut and shook the memory away. I had tufts of grass that needed to be cut.

I noticed, after sitting there for an hour or two, that several women had gathered in the shade of a tree and seemed to be watching me. Staring right at me. Every once in a while, they'd lean toward one another to speak or laugh, but most of the time, they stood silently, just *staring*.

I got a lot of scratches on my hands, more than my share, from the sharp edges of the leaves, so I decided to take a break to go inside for a thorough hand washing with my antibacterial soap and then maybe a bandage or two. Mr. Cirone grimaced when I showed him my hands, and he warned me to be more careful in the future.

I said, "Well, those women are making me nervous."

"What women?"

When I turned to point them out to him, though, the place beside the tree where they had been standing was empty. "Never mind," I said, and walked inside the house.

Mr. Marsh had fallen asleep lying on top of his sleeping bag, and Judah was still asleep inside his. The house was quiet and cooler than outside. How tempting, to lie down and close my eyes. I'd gotten almost no sleep the past two days and nights, and weariness seemed to catch up with me all at once in the stillness of a few inactive moments.

But as soon as Mrs. Cirone finished cleaning my hands, smearing antibacterial ointment all over them, and wrapping them in gauze, I freed my hair from the clip I'd had it in all day, brushed it, and pulled it up in a ponytail. Then, telling myself I could sleep later, I went back outside.

We worked until Mr. Cirone left to go buy dinner, but I was so exhausted by then that I fell asleep before he returned with it and didn't wake up again until dawn.

Cool, restful dawn.

I stood and stepped carefully over Hope and Callie on my way outside. The pale blue sky was cloudless, but everything looked as if rain had fallen on it. Water dripped on my hair from branches, leaves, and ferns that hung deep green and heavy with morning dew. For several minutes, I stood perfectly still behind Mr. Meyer's house, listening to the jungle around me and watching a bird poking its beak repeatedly into a puddle of water on a huge leaf near the ground.

As I stood there, I began to hear noises from the other side of the house, so slowly, and as silently as I could, I walked to the wall and crept along it until I could just see the front of the house around the corner.

The same group of women who'd been staring at me the day before were setting bowls of food and baskets of tiny bread loaves on the bench near the door! I recognized one of them. The mother of the little boy I'd helped in the plaza!

Before I could decide whether or not to step around the corner and reveal myself to them, they hurried back into the jungle and were gone. I walked to the front of the house, picked up two of the bowls of food, and went inside to wake Mr. Cirone.

He woke everyone, and we sat in a circle on the floor to eat.

I helped myself to two servings of scrambled eggs, half a papaya—a huge yellow one—and bread. Every bite was delicious. And there was plenty. We all ate our fill and then some.

"Should I thank the women if I see them today?" I asked Mr. Cirone.

"No," he said. "We don't want to put anyone in danger if people are watching them." He smiled. "I couldn't even get us breakfast yesterday. I'm sure those women know how grateful we are."

"Do you think it'll be safe for them soon?" Matt asked.

Mr. Cirone answered slowly. Quietly. "If Dane gets through to help."

"How will we know if . . . if he doesn't?"

Again, Mr. Cirone didn't answer right away. "We'll give him some time. We've got up to ten days that we can stay here before we have to head out. If he's not back by then with help, we'll have to assume he—"

"He'll be here," Shane said.

Mr. Cirone nodded. "I hope so."

Nobody wanted to discuss it any further.

We worked on the church building through the cool of early morning and well into the heat of the day without taking any breaks. My job was to help hold the support poles in place while several of the boys shoveled and packed dirt in around them to steady them. This work was a lot more motivating—though less challenging—than the work I'd done the day before. I liked it because I could see the results of my labor right away. By the time we rested for lunch, Shane, Chad, Rebekah, and I had put up three poles, another team of four had put up three more, and the third team had only the two in the center of the church left. Mr. Cirone told us that we should be able to complete the building in seven or eight days if we continued to work so well together and so diligently.

A week.

Would Mr. Meyer be back to see his church finished? If not, would we have built it for nothing?

Lord, please protect him, I prayed, though I didn't know if I really believed that He would . . . or even could. Please.

For three days, we worked on the church. Hot days. Stagnant days. No word from Mr. Meyer. Tedious and monotonous work. Packing in the mud and stone *cimiento* all along the perimeter of the building. Covering the roof structure with the palm leaves and placing it atop the support beams. Adding bamboo poles to the wall, one at a time, side by side, and weaving the vines around them in three places—near the top, near the bottom, and in the middle.

Looking toward the jungle one afternoon, at all the trees—real logs—I asked Mr. Cirone why the people here used bamboo poles for their buildings instead of wood.

He grinned. "Ever try chopping down a tree with a machete, Miss Cook?"

"No. But couldn't they get saws and other tools up here?"

"Even if they could," he answered, "wood is so valuable in Mexico that these people would sell any tree they cut down—provide for their family for a whole year—rather than build their house with it."

I grabbed another pole without another word.

Long days.

We made no progress with the people in the village. Except for the women who brought us breakfast each morning, the people still kept away from us, making us wonder whether they even wanted the church that we were working so hard to build. Mr.

Cirone continued to remind us that fear, like the local drug trafficker himself, was a powerful and competent enemy. We shouldn't resent the people's distancing themselves from us. In their situation—if we could even begin to place ourselves there—wouldn't we behave exactly as they had?

What I found myself asking, though, was how Mr. Meyer had endured more than a year here among these people before the first of them came to Christ. How had he kept himself from surrendering to discouragement? From questioning his discernment of God's will. From depression. Resentment. The feeling of uselessness.

"He must have kept his eyes on God instead of on how things looked," Rebekah said when I mentioned some of my thoughts to her. She, Shane, Judah, and Hope and I were washing the dinner dishes in the pail behind Mr. Meyer's house.

"But how did he know it was God he was looking at, and not just his own idea of how God wanted him to serve Him?"

"Well . . . people did eventually get saved," Hope said.

"Yes," I said, "and now they're fearful for their lives."

Rebekah shrugged. "That doesn't mean Mr. Meyer wasn't supposed to come here."

"We're Americans," Judah said. "Most of us have never been persecuted for our faith—other than some kid who sees us praying in the lunchroom or an evolutionist who laughs at us in science class. But Christians in other parts of the world *are* persecuted. Do you think God would rather these people never accepted Christ so that they wouldn't have to be fearful for their lives now?"

"No," I said.

"And I bet you none of them would either," Shane said.

Chapter 12

The drumming of rain on the thatched roof woke me the next morning. It was the first time since arriving in Mr. Meyer's village that I'd actually slept later than sunrise, but I was still the first one awake. I rolled onto my side and tried to go back to sleep, but the noise of the rain, the warm humidity, and the grumbling of my stomach kept me up. Rather than lying awake and thinking, I got up and ran to the outhouse as fast as I could so that I wouldn't get soaked. Then I gathered up the breakfast the women had left for us and carried it inside. They had covered everything with cloths, but they'd obviously been up a lot earlier than I had. The eggs had gone lukewarm and the bread soggy, but I doubted that anyone would complain.

I dug in my pack through several sets of dirty clothes in search of the least offensive and went to the curtained-off corner of the room to change into them.

Mr. Cirone had allotted us time this morning to wash our clothes, and in spite of washboard, rocks, and pouring rain, I couldn't wait to get started. Putting dirty clothes back on was something I'd never before had to do.

As people woke, ate breakfast, and took turns behind the curtain changing clothes, the rain began to beat less incessantly on the roof, diminishing to a light plinking and finally stopping altogether. Two at a time, while the rest of the team resumed working on the church building, we took our laundry out behind the house and hand washed it with dark brown bar soap, *IBIS,* in a bucket of water each pair had to haul up themselves. Mr. Cirone stretched ropes from tree to tree, where we could hang the clothes to dry—which he warned us might take a couple of days.

"Who'd have thought laundry could be so much work," Rebekah muttered, rubbing her wrists after we finished. "My arms hurt more from wringing everything out than they ever do after working on the church."

I dumped our water. "It's worth it to have clean clothes again."

"That's for sure."

We handed the bucket off to Hope and Callie and took their positions helping Judah and Shane put poles up between two of the support beams on the south side of the building. Holding the bamboo poles in place was easy enough—they were light. Weaving the vines through and around each of them was a bit trickier, especially when Mr. Cirone decided that we needed a horizontal beam halfway up to provide added stability to the wall. He nailed long planks of wood from support beam to support beam, which we would wrap the vine around every time we set a bamboo pole in place against it.

For most of the morning, my job was to hold the poles while Shane twisted a vine around the bottom, Rebekah labored with the middle, and Judah reached to secure the top. They struggled, at first, to keep out of each other's way, but quickly devised a routine that suited them. Still, all that time on our feet combined with the almost suffocating heat began to wear on us. Shane started speaking to Judah in terse two- and three-word sentences. "Back off!" "Wait, will you?" "So long."

If, for some reason, I failed to stand the next pole in place quickly enough for Shane, or was still rotating it for the snuggest fit against the pole beside it when he was ready to start tightening the vine around them, he glared up at me as if I had spinach for brains and would have served God and humanity better by staying at home.

I kept telling him to relax. Rebekah tried to remain cheerful in spite of him. Judah just got quiet. He stopped complimenting our efforts. He stopped reminding Rebekah to take care about avoiding splinters as she looped vines around the unsanded wood board. And when he accidentally dropped one of the poles on Shane's foot, he barely managed an apology.

That wasn't like him.

Rebekah noticed too. "Judah, do you need a break?"

"He needs more than that," Shane muttered.

"You know what?" Judah looked at Shane. "I do need a break." He walked quickly away from us toward Mr. Meyer's house.

Grateful for the break myself, I pulled off the work gloves Mr. Cirone had loaned me because I'd scratched my hands so badly and pushed past Shane, bumping him a little harder than I had to. "Nice attitude, macho man."

"I'm sorry," he said. "I guess I was kind of a jerk."

"Kind of?" I elbowed him.

"Don't press me." He smiled. "Or I might change my mind about giving you *that* much."

I grinned up at him. "*I'm* not the one you should be giving it to, anyway."

"I know." Shane shoved his hands in his pockets and looked down at the dirt. Clearly, he wasn't looking forward to apologizing to Judah. "What was with Ewen, anyway? The last hour or so, he was acting like the vines weighed a thousand pounds each!"

"Oh, come on, Shane," I said. "That's what you're going to tell your church back home when you do your Mission Report, isn't it? 'We built a church in three-hundred-degree weather by braiding vines through and around bamboo poles narrower than pencils . . . thousands of them . . . all with our bare hands!' Admit it."

He laughed. "Yeah. Right."

We walked to Mr. Meyer's house and ate lunch with the rest of the team. Nobody chatted much, or ate much, but everyone gulped down at least two glassfuls of the rainwater we'd collected in that morning's downpour. Lukewarm, but refreshing. Then, too soon, we headed back to the church in the same groups of four.

Shane cleared his throat. "Hey, Ewen, I'm sorry for cutting you down all morning."

"No problem," Judah said.

"Well, anyway, I'm sorry."

Judah said nothing.

"Are you feeling okay?" Shane asked him.

"Okay enough."

"Because nobody'll think any less of you if you need to take the afternoon off."

Rebekah agreed.

"*I'll* think less of me," Judah insisted. "I didn't come here to laze around Mr. Meyer's house while all of you do all the work." He looked at Rebekah. "Besides, I feel okay today. I mean, it's hot, my shoulders are sore, and the wood is tearing my hands apart . . . but, you know, all of us are putting up with those things." He smiled. "Please don't treat me like death is imminent. Mrs. Cirone has been doing enough of that for all of you. More than my mother would, even."

We all grinned and nodded. Mrs. Cirone treated every case of food intolerance, every scratch, every unusual insect bite, and every poisonous plant or human encounter as if it could be fatal if not checked on the hour every hour. Though the remoteness of our location and the dangers of the environment did demand caution, Mrs. Cirone's attention seemed . . . well, Judah had said it . . . more overprotective than a mother's. But she'd told us that they'd nearly lost a girl on a trip to a different area of Mexico—because of a scorpion sting—so we let her tend to us in whatever way she saw fit.

When we arrived back at our portion of the wall, we started right in on getting to work. We knew that if we worked efficiently enough, we might finish our section of the church by the end of the day, and that motivated us. Through the heat. In spite of the sore muscles. Past the pain in our palms and the annoying sting of sweat mixed with sunscreen dripping into our eyes.

We could finish this.

Five more sections of the wall hadn't even been started yet, but *this* part could be finished.

Toward the end of the afternoon when it felt like we'd been working for too many hours, Rebekah, who had switched jobs with me, refused to go to the stack for any more poles. She sat in the shade of the partly finished wall and said, "Sorry, guys. I need a break. It's way too hot."

"No complaints here." Judah sat beside her. "Come on, Shane. Get out of the sun for a while."

Shane stood beside the pile of poles we had not yet put up. "We won't finish if we take a break now." His tone was as tense as his expression.

I shoved my disorderly mess of vines out of the way so that I could sit down. "A hundred years from now," I said, "who's going to care if we finish today or tomorrow?"

Judah leaned forward and rested his forehead on his knees. "I don't think it even matters *now*."

"It matters to me," Shane insisted.

"Well, it shouldn't."

Rebekah, Judah, and I sat in the shade for several minutes, not speaking; we were feeling—but trying to ignore—Shane's anger as he kicked at the sand at his feet. But when he asked, "So, how long do you plan to sit there like one of the girls, Ewen?" Rebekah had had enough. She got stiffly to her feet, stepped toward Shane, stood on her toes when she got there so that she could put her face right up to within an inch of his, and said, "I'm done sitting here, Shane. I'm going to go sit in Mr. Meyer's house. Cool off. Get a drink of water. Wash my face. Be human. I hope that's okay with you, because if it isn't, that's just too bad."

I sat there, stunned. I'd seen Rebekah display some feistiness a couple of times, but never an all-out attitude. Apparently, she didn't appreciate Shane's attempt to deride Judah. Strangely, neither did I. Each of us had probably worked off ten pounds from the sweat and skin off our palms that day, and nobody deserved to be made to feel lazy because there were still a few poles to put up.

"Well," I said, "I guess we're done for the day." I stood and dusted the sand off the back of my jeans. "We'll finish tomorrow, Shane. It's no big deal."

He refused even to look at me.

Rebekah held her hand out to Judah. "Come on. It's got to be at least a little cooler inside Mr. Meyer's house."

Judah didn't move. He just stared at Rebekah and me with an expression as vacant as the inside cover of a paperback book.

I grinned as I lightly knocked twice on his head. "Hello?"

"Funny," he mumbled. "You're a regular comedian."

His words sounded slurred, almost. Emotionless. Rebekah sat beside him. "Are you okay?"

"I'm hot."

That was evident enough. *Aren't we all?*

But Rebekah said, "Judah, what's wrong?"

"I'm hot," he repeated. "It's too hot."

Looking somewhat frightened, Rebekah touched the side of Judah's face with the back of her hand. "Shane," she said quickly, "go get Mrs. Cirone."

Judah didn't protest . . . which frightened me.

It must have scared Shane too. He bolted toward Mr. Meyer's house, calling for Mrs. Cirone.

Chapter 13

"This happens." Mrs. Cirone dipped a clean cloth into the bucket of cold water Mr. Marsh had run to get for her, wrung it out, and began to press at Judah's face and neck with it. "People get sick. They dehydrate. The heat gets to them sooner." She shook her head. "We've just got to cool him down, get him to drink plenty of fluids, and he'll be fine." She wrung out the cloth again.

"I'm sorry." Judah looked first at Mrs. Cirone and then past her at her husband, who was standing near one of the windows. "You told me not to overdo it. It's just . . . we were so close to finishing our part of the building, and I really didn't feel that bad until I sat down."

"Don't apologize." Mr. Cirone stared down at Judah. "We shouldn't have given you the opportunity to overdo it."

After glancing at Mr. Cirone with one of those *What am I . . . a first grader?* looks, Judah apologized again. "I should have stopped sooner."

"Yes, you should have!" Mrs. Cirone's smile told the truth about the obviously exaggerated sternness in her tone. "Stop talking now and get some sleep."

Judah had no trouble following *that* instruction.

While Mrs. Cirone stayed inside the house with Judah, the rest of us went to buy dinner. Even though Mrs. Cirone had assured us that Judah would be fine, there was a shortage of the usual half-joking, half-serious whining about the day's work, as well as of any other conversation. Everyone seemed distracted . . . stilled, like me, by how quickly things could have turned scary and out of control. I heard several kids commenting about their not-quite-recognized-until-now appreciation for the competent and caring adults who had sacrificed any chance they may have had at a relaxing summer to take the bunch of us on this trip.

I stepped up beside Rebekah. "He'll be okay," I said. "Mrs. Cirone knows what she's doing."

"I know." But she didn't look consoled at all. "I guess I just wish I had insisted on taking a break sooner."

I nodded. That probably would have made a difference. "But," I said, "he has a mouth. He could have asked for a break."

"Yeah . . . " She shrugged.

"I know." I laughed. "He and Shane had some kind of guy thing going on about getting finished."

"Exactly." Rebekah grinned.

We caught up with the rest of the group as Mr. Cirone paid the old man for our food. Rebekah and I had just stepped past the market's open doorway into the shade when we had to turn around and head back outside onto the hot plaza.

"Let's go eat at the spring," Callie suggested.

Mr. Cirone nodded his consent and led us toward the trail down to the river. "Anyone feeling sick yet?" he asked.

Earlier that morning, Matt and Alec had taken a wrong turn on the twisting and narrow trail down to the river where we'd been getting our laundry water and had accidentally, if not miraculously, stumbled over a natural spring. The water pouring from it was clear and cold, and Mr. Cirone had allowed a few people to drink it to see if it would make anyone sick. So far, it hadn't.

"I'm fine," Shane said.

"I feel good," reported Matt.

Callie nodded. "Me too."

"So do I," said Mr. Cirone. "Spring water is usually safer because its source isn't polluted, but I don't want us drinking more of it until I know for sure. If nobody is sick by morning, we can drink all we want."

"So, why are we going to the spring then?" Shane asked.

"Because it's cooler there than in Dane's house, and it's been a long, hot day."

Nobody protested that.

Huge ferns, as green as green could be imagined, grew all around the area where the spring came out of the ground. We sat among them, shooing away more insects than anyone wanted to count, and ate our dinner. The sound of the water, the sight of it, the coolness of the air, and even the smell of the place, relaxed me. We stayed there long after everyone had finished eating, enjoying the stillness. A couple of kids fell asleep. Mr. Cirone told us more of his mission team stories. The night began to cool and darken.

"I want to go back to Mr. Meyer's house." Rebekah stood and looked at Mr. Cirone. "May I?"

"I can't believe she wasn't saying that two hours ago," Hope whispered to Callie.

"Neither can I!"

Shane glared at both of them. "I'll take her," he said to Mr. Cirone.

Mr. Cirone nodded.

Nobody spoke after Shane and Rebekah had gone.

I thought of Mr. Meyer.

Finally, Mr. Cirone stood and brushed off his pants. "I guess we all might as well head back. It'll be dark—"

A shout from the jungle behind him interrupted him. "Mr. Cirone!"

Mr. Cirone turned toward the path and raised his arm just in time to keep Shane from running into him. "What is it?" he demanded.

"Mrs. Cirone needs you," he answered breathlessly. He spun around and headed back up the path, but not before all of us saw the panic in his eyes.

Mr. Cirone didn't stop him to ask for an explanation. He just followed him, running, toward Mr. Meyer's house, waving to the rest of us to follow him.

We did.

Up the trail. Out onto the plaza. Across it.

I noticed that a couple of people stopped what they were doing to stare curiously at us as we rushed by them. Some of the children stepped forward to follow us but were held back by their mothers.

When we pulled open Mr. Meyer's door and crowded inside, Mrs. Cirone got to her feet and looked straight at her husband as if the rest of us weren't even there. "We have a problem," she said.

"I figured as much," Mr. Cirone said. "What is it?"

"Come here." Mrs. Cirone approached Judah, who was lying on his stomach on top of his sleeping bag. She knelt beside him and nodded to Rebekah to lift the wet cloth she was holding on Judah's shoulder.

She did.

Behind me, Callie pulled in a sharp breath and raised her hand to her mouth. In front of me, Mr. Cirone looked up at the ceiling and then sat beside his wife. Suddenly cold, I shoved my hands in my pockets and straightened my arms so that they were tight against my sides.

On Judah's back, about two inches down from the base of his neck and just to the left of his spine, his skin was swollen and discolored all around a thick black mark.

"What is it?" someone behind me whispered.

"Judah?" Mr. Cirone asked, his voice tense, "what did you scratch yourself on?"

Mrs. Cirone answered for Judah because he seemed to be only half awake. "He doesn't know for sure."

I remembered Judah getting to his feet after that boy had hit him with the plank of wood, the day my sack was stolen. He'd been rubbing at the back of his left shoulder as I walked toward him, hadn't he?

Yes. He had.

Mr. Cirone leaned closer to Judah and, louder now, asked, "How long has your shoulder been hurting you?"

Judah didn't answer right away. "Since we hiked in here, I think."

"That long?" Mr. Cirone shut his eyes while he rubbed at his temples for a moment. "It's been hurting you *that long* and you didn't say anything? What were you—"

Gently, Mrs. Cirone placed her hand on her husband's arm and shook her head.

"I thought I'd done something to it backpacking, sir," Judah said. "And then working on the church . . . I didn't think . . ."

I tried to remember . . . When Judah had pulled his hand away from his neck, had there been blood on his hand?

Had there?

"All right," Mr. Cirone said. "All right. You scratched yourself on something that must have been very dirty, Judah, but it's okay." He looked at his wife. "We're going to have to clean it."

She nodded.

There had been blood on Judah's hand that day in the street.

But it could have gotten there when he'd pulled the boy away from me. He could have hit one of them.

"I need boiled water," Mrs. Cirone said. "Clean cloths. I need someone to sterilize a small knife."

"This is probably the reason he's been sick, and not that snow cone he ate." Mr. Cirone breathed out through his lips as he pulled his hand away from Judah's forehead. "He's burning up."

I took an unintentional step backwards.

"This is going to hurt him." After Mrs. Cirone had gathered everything she needed, she looked at those of us standing closest to her. "Ashton, Hope, come and help Rebekah hold him so that he can't jerk away from me."

Hope stepped forward to help, but I couldn't move. I couldn't even open my mouth to say *no*. I just stood there.

Shane stared curiously at me, and then pushed by me to help in my place.

This was *my* fault. Oh, I hadn't smacked Judah with that two-by-four, but I may as well have. *I* had been the one to suggest that we leave the plaza. *I* had put us in the path of those boys. I said, "Mr. Cirone?"

He looked over his shoulder, clearly not appreciating my interruption just now.

But I had to. "That day we left the plaza and my stuff was stolen?"

Mr. Cirone nodded.

"When Judah pulled the boys away from me . . ."

Mr. Cirone—everyone—looked at me, waiting.

I swallowed. "One of them hit him with a piece of wood across the back. It must have . . . something must have been poking out of it because . . ."

"It doesn't really matter what scratched him, Miss Cook," Mr. Cirone said quietly after several silent moments. "What matters is that we take care of it."

Chapter 14

Mrs. Cirone sat beside me on the bench in front of Mr. Meyer's house. She covered her face with the towel she'd been using to dry her hands and leaned her head back against the wall. It had taken her nearly an hour to clean all the infection out of Judah's shoulder, and she'd spent at least as long again sitting beside him until he fell asleep.

I'd come outside before she'd finished with the cut because it felt like a knife in my stomach every time I saw Judah tense against the pain. I'd pushed so quickly past the door when I'd come out that I'd frightened away a couple of children who must have been peering through the window.

"Are you all right?" I asked, unable to look at Mrs. Cirone.

"I'm okay."

"Is Judah?"

"I've done everything I can do for him tonight," she said. "He'll have to be taken to Poza Rica as soon as it's light in the morning."

"How will—?"

"Some of the guys will have to carry him out."

I pulled away when I felt her hand on my forearm.

"This isn't your fault, Ashton," she said.

Without warning, though I supposed they'd been threatening all night, tears came, and I was helpless against them. I leaned forward, put my face in my hands, and tried to will them away, but they wouldn't obey me. "Is he going to be all right?" I'd inadvertently interrupted Mrs. Cirone's attempt to tell me again that this wasn't my fault. Or had I done it purposely? Either way, it worked. She didn't finish the sentence. I asked again, "Is he going to be all right?"

"He's running a pretty high fever." She leaned slightly forward. "That could just be because of the infection . . ."

"But?"

"But," she said, "it's more likely because the infection has spread into his bloodstream. He'll need antibiotics, if so." She placed her hand on my shoulder. "We'll get him to Poza Rica. He'll be okay." After squeezing my shoulder twice, she stood and stepped back inside.

A half an hour passed. An hour.

So many feelings piled in on me. Strong. Noisy. Raw. And this time, all my attempts to ignore, refuse, or distract myself from them failed. I felt ashamed. I felt guilty. I felt confused about feeling guilty . . . Judah was responsible for my brother's death, so why should I feel guilty that he'd been hurt on account of me?

But I'd never allowed myself to decide whether or not I really believed that Tommy's death was Judah's fault. It hurt too much. If it was Judah's fault, then I'd want to hate him, and I'd lose a brother *and* a friend. If it wasn't Judah's fault . . . well, then I'd have to blame Tommy for being careless enough to risk taking the shortcut in high, fast water. And if it wasn't Tommy's fault, if it was just a random accident . . . then I'd be forced to ask God why He'd allowed it to happen. I'd never wanted to be angry. At Judah. Or Tommy. Or God. So I'd found ways to just not think about it. And, for two years, that had worked.

But it was a lie. It wasn't real healing. Or real peace.

People had been impressed by my strength. By my ability to move on in spite of what had happened to my brother. By the fact that I'd never hated Judah Ewen out loud—though I'd endured some criticism about that from several people, including Chad Reese.

"He doesn't deserve for you to forgive him. Your brother's dead because of him. What's wrong with you?"

Now, as I sat alone on a bench in front of a house in the middle of a jungle, I realized that what Chad and others had mistaken for forgiveness and strength on my part had really only been avoidance. Hiding, as Mrs. Cirone had said. I didn't blame him. I didn't not blame him. I just didn't think about it.

Being here in Mexico with Judah Ewen hadn't been easy at every moment, but it hadn't been difficult or painful either. Not the way I would have expected it to be had I known he'd be here. The way it had been for Chad.

It had simply been . . . numb. He was here. I was here. Why think about it . . . just live with it. And that's what I'd done.

"You can't just expect to shove it all inside and be over it. That's not how you heal."

The sound of the door shutting startled me, and I looked toward it as Chad stepped outside and sat beside me.

"How are you doing?" he asked me.

"I don't know."

"This isn't your fault, Ashton," he said. "And even if it—"

"No." I stood and walked a few steps away from the bench, into the darkness. "Chad, no. You've decided to blame Judah for Tommy's death. You hate him. I know that. So, of course it doesn't bother you all that much that he's lying in there burning up. But I . . . I haven't decided whether or not I blame him. I don't hate him. And . . . and even if I do blame him . . . I don't think God would want me to hate him. Maybe he doesn't deserve my forgiveness, but . . ." I thought of my own sins and how I could take them to Jesus and be assured of His forgiveness. "Is forgiveness ever deserved?"

It was several moments before he answered. "No."

I walked slowly back to the bench and sat down. "Chad," I said, "I have a lot of stuff I have to think through right now. Stuff I've been shoving inside since Tommy's death. I don't want to hide from it anymore. I want to *really* move on." I looked right at him and hoped he wouldn't be offended. "I need to do that by myself."

He nodded, stood up, and went back inside.

I sat there a long time. I didn't know how long. Letting myself think. Letting myself cry. Letting myself ask God why. Letting myself remember Tommy, and that horrible day at the river when we'd found his body, and the way I'd wanted to feel the day the Ewens left.

I sat there . . . until a noise in the trees beside me startled me so that I jumped to my feet without thinking first. Nobody had come out of the house other than Mrs. Cirone and Chad, and yet I could feel someone near me. Someone whose silhouette I could barely see in the shadows of the leaves beyond the light coming from the window beside me.

I didn't bother asking *Who's there?* Nobody in this place spoke English, and it was obvious that this person probably wouldn't answer even if he or she did.

I moved toward the door.

The silhouette moved with me. Something wet and warm pressed against my arm.

What . . . ?

The person pushed it more firmly against me.

I reached up and grabbed it, intending to also grab hold of the person's hand and find out what this was all about, but the leaves rustled and the silhouette disappeared as soon as my hands touched whatever it was that I was now holding. Warm. Wet. A bundle of something the size and shape of a pound of ground beef wrapped in cloth. It smelled like a giant teabag, one of those herbal varieties my mother was always drinking.

I took it inside. "Somebody gave this to me."

Mrs. Cirone stood and took it instantly. Gratefully.

"What is it?" I asked.

"It's a poultice," she said. "Medicine around here is pretty primitive, but I've seen things like this work wonders." She knelt beside Judah, removed the cloth that was on his back, and replaced it with the poultice. She placed Rebekah's hand on top of it and told her to make sure it stayed put. "People use certain combinations of ground plants, bark, nuts, or whatever, to remedy all kinds of things."

"But how did they know about Judah?" Rebekah asked.

"I don't know," Mrs. Cirone said.

The children who'd been looking through the window! Maybe they had run and told their mothers. Maybe one of those mothers knew how to make these poultices. Maybe Judah would be okay without having to go all the way to Poza Rica.

"Will it help him?" Rebekah asked.

Again, "I don't know."

"It can't hurt, though . . . right?"

Mrs. Cirone nodded at the concern in Rebekah's eyes. "No. It can't hurt. It might help the pain a little."

"We've still got to take him out of here in the morning." Mr. Cirone looked up from the two pack frames he was trying to tie together. "It's seven miles to the van," he said. "Judah probably weighs, what, 170 or 175 pounds?" He thought for a moment. "Four of us will have to go. Two teams to take turns carrying him. Three of you and either Mr. Marsh or I. I haven't decided that yet."

"I'll go," Shane quickly volunteered.

Quietly, Chad did the same.

I glanced at him curiously for several seconds. Then I looked at Mr. Marsh. His expression was apprehensive . . . and I couldn't blame him. He was either going to suddenly be in charge of a bunch of kids here in the village while we finished the church, or he was going to have the task of seeing to it that Judah made it to a doctor—a good one—fast enough.

"Sir?" Rebekah waited for Mr. Cirone to look at her. "I hope you don't think I'm staying here?"

He opened his mouth to reply—and from the seriousness of his expression I deduced that his answer was not going to be the one Rebekah wanted to hear—but a quiet tap at Mr. Meyer's door interrupted him.

We all looked at him, uneasy.

He nodded to Mr. Marsh, who went to open the door.

Three men and one woman, all of whom I had seen many times in the plaza, stared in at us. One of the men spoke to Mr. Cirone in Spanish, who then hurried to let them in. The three men stayed near the door, speaking quietly and quickly with Mr. Cirone, while the woman went to Judah and lifted the poultice. She inspected the cut and the job Mrs. Cirone had done of cleaning it, and then, closing her eyes, whispered something. Gently, she replaced the poultice and then stood to rejoin the men by the door.

One of the men, after staring long at the wall, addressed Mr. Cirone. Even though I couldn't understand a word he was saying, his urgent tone, his rushed speech, and his frequent hand movements plainly revealed his distress about Judah's condition.

And then, as quickly as they had come, the strangers left.

In response to our puzzled expressions, Mr. Cirone sat down and said, "Those three men are going to help us get Judah down as soon as it's light." He looked at Mr. Marsh. "With you." He turned to Shane, Chad, and Matt, the other boy who had volunteered to help. "Thanks for being willing to help, but it's better that more of us will be staying here." Then he looked at Rebekah. "I'm sorry, Rebekah, but it's safer for you to stay here—"

"But—"

"—with the rest of us. I don't want to put more responsibility on Mr. Marsh than he'll already have with Judah." He raised his hand when Rebekah started to protest again. He had made his decision.

And Rebekah stiffened accordingly. She was furious. "I need to go to the outhouse." She stood and started walking toward the door.

Toward me.

I stepped aside, making certain I wouldn't be in her path, and stared down at my feet.

She stopped beside me. I could feel her there, defiant like the cold of an Alaska night. "Coming?"

As I looked up and turned my head to face her, I noticed that Mr. and Mrs. Cirone had both stopped what they were doing just then to glance at us. But I was Rebekah's partner. Nobody was supposed to go away from the house alone. So, unnerved or not, I followed her outside.

She's got to hate me. If only I hadn't insisted on leaving the plaza to buy that stupid wallet!

We walked through the dark toward the outhouse.

"Since we're alone," she said, "I want to tell you now that I don't blame you for Judah being sick." She kept talking even as I told her that I wouldn't blame her if she did. "Yes, it was you who first wanted to leave the plaza. But it's not your fault that one of those kids picked up a two-by-four and hit Judah with it. It's not your fault that it was dirty. It just . . . happened that way."

"Thanks," I said. I appreciated her attitude, especially since her emotions had to be ragged knowing that she'd have to let Judah go in the morning and then spend the next several days in agonized waiting. "Thanks."

When we got back to Mr. Meyer's house and Rebekah had gone inside, I sat on the bench again, alone, and stared blankly past the shadows of our nearly built church and out across the blackness of the sleeping plaza.

I still had a lot of thinking to do.

Chapter 15

I woke up gasping, clutching the edge of the bench in front of Mr. Meyer's house, my heart pounding. The nightmare. Even in the middle of the night, the jungle air pressed warm against me, much warmer than the air had been that day at the river a little more than two years ago. But it did not comfort me. I was freezing.

Quickly, I stood to go inside the house. I leaned against the wall and waited for my pulse to slow to normal and my trembling to stop.

As I stood there, I noticed that I had not been the only one to fall asleep outside. Mrs. Cirone must have come out to check on me at some point and, instead of waking me, sat on the bench beside me. Glad that I hadn't awakened her—she had to be exhausted—I stepped quietly past the bench and inside the house.

In the dim light cast by the oil lamp on the table, I saw Mr. Cirone and Rebekah, both asleep sitting beside Judah . . . who was awake. Shivering.

Carefully, I stepped over three people, bent to pick up my sleeping bag, and carried it over another three people before kneeling beside Judah to cover him with it. I knew that his shivering meant that his temperature was rising and that I probably should be trying to cool him down rather than putting a sleeping bag over him. But I also knew that my mother's quilt always seemed like much better medicine when I had chills than a cold cloth on the back.

"Thanks," he said. "What time is it?"

I moved my arm around at every conceivable angle, but could not make out the time on my watch in the dim light. "I don't know. Late." I smiled. "Or early."

He turned stiffly onto his side and pulled his knees up. "I feel like such a loser."

"Why?"

"Because I'm causing all this trouble, and it's just a stupid little scratch."

I rested the palm of my hand against his face. *Hot.* "It's not your fault," I said. "I'm the one who—"

"Don't." He backed away from my hand on his face. "Don't."

"You're so sick," I whispered.

"It's not your fault."

He had barely whispered it, but it stung me as if he had shouted. Not because of the words themselves, exactly, but because they stood in painful contrast to so many words that had been spoken to him.

"Judah?"

"Uh-huh."

"I'm sorry."

"I told you," he said, "it's not your—"

"No, Judah. I mean I'm sorry for the way things happened after Tommy's death. I'm sorry for being too afraid to deal with it then. I'm sorry I couldn't have told you I didn't blame you, or that I forgave you if I did blame you."

"Ash—"

"Wait." If I had planned this moment out, or even imagined it to be possible, I had no doubt that I would have predicted tears, and guilt, and shame. But strangely, I felt nothing but *rightness* about it. "It was wrong of people to believe all this time that Tommy would be alive for sure right now if you had gone with him that day."

Now I began to feel the pressure of tears at my eyes. "Nobody can know that. Tommy's dying was hard enough. Terrible enough. And all everyone did was make it harder. For all of us." I wiped at my eyes. "I know you might think I'm saying all this just because I feel guilty about your being sick. Because it was my idea to leave the plaza, and none of this would have happened if we hadn't. I *do* feel bad. And, see, *that's* the point. That's what makes me know that the only sane thing to do is move on. Because if I really hated you the way I thought I should hate you, if I really believed that you were responsible for my brother's death, I don't think I'd feel this way." Suddenly nervous, I shook my head. "Do you understand?"

His reply came slowly, one word at a time, as if he were listening to each word after he spoke it, making sure he believed it. "Sometimes, Ashton, I don't even understand what's inside *me*. I might not understand everything you're feeling right now . . ." He laughed. "I can't even see straight right now." His expression went serious again. "But I do believe you. And I forgive you. I had to forgive you a long time ago or there would have been no peace."

Placing my hand against his face again, I shut my eyes and did something I had expected never to do again. I prayed for Judah Ewen. His face felt so hot beneath my hand that I decided, once he'd fallen asleep again, to pull the sleeping bag down away from his shoulders. Comforting medicine or not, a cold cloth on the back was what he needed.

Morning crept slowly in through the windows and all the spaces between the mismatched poles of the house. At some point during those hours, I fell asleep. When I woke up—with my face on my knees and my hand still over the cloth on Judah's forehead, I was surprised to see the full strength of sunrise in the windows . . . and not to feel heat beneath my hand. Sitting up straight, I lifted the cloth so that I could press the back of my hand directly against Judah's face. I held it there for several seconds. Then I moved it to the back of his neck.

"His fever's down," I told Rebekah. I shook her fully awake. "Maybe even gone."

When Mrs. Cirone confirmed this with a thermometer, all three of us smiled in relief. Mr. Cirone, however, responded less enthusiastically. After waking Judah, helping him sit up, and handing him a cup of water, he asked, "Are you feeling any better?"

Judah quickly drank the water. "Yes, sir."

"I still want you to go down and have that infection checked out."

Grabbing his boots, Judah nodded.

Mr. Cirone chuckled. "Go ahead and put those on, if you like, but you're not walking anywhere."

"Sir . . ." Judah glanced at the make-do stretcher leaning against the wall and then stared up at Mr. Cirone. He finished tying his boots without a word, apparently perceiving that arguing would be pointless, but his expression demonstrated his mortification plainly enough.

Struggling not to laugh, Rebekah moved toward him to console him. "Judah, do you really feel up to walking seven miles?"

Judah fumed a bit before answering. "Even if I don't, I don't need to be *carried!*"

Callie giggled. "Ah, the male ego." Then she opened the door for the three men who'd come to help Mr. Marsh get Judah down to the bottom of the trail.

I didn't laugh at Callie's comment with the rest of the kids. I understood how Judah felt . . . there was nothing uniquely male about wanting to carry your own weight—literally, in this case—so as not to be a burden to others.

Most of us waited outside while Mr. and Mrs. Cirone readied Judah for the hike down. Morning in the jungle truly was beautiful. Mist clung to the treetops. The dense and pleasantly warm air seemed alive with rich and tropical scents from so many dew-drenched plants. And, everywhere, *green* that hadn't grown droopy yet with the heat of the day.

We noticed several groups of people standing in or near the plaza, all of them looking our way. We sat on Mr. Meyer's bench, or stood in quiet groups near the front of the house, and pretended not to feel watched.

Within minutes, the door opened and two of the three men from the village carried Judah outside. He squinted against the shrouded but still potent brightness of the sky and muttered something about sunglasses.

Smiling, I squeezed his hand. "Stay better, okay?"

"I will."

Rebekah followed Mr. Marsh out of the house. "You'd better," she said. She took Judah's hand when I let it go, but the vigorous pace of the men walking, combined with Mrs. Cirone's hand on Rebekah's shoulder—reminding her that she wasn't going anywhere—forced her to let go again sooner than either she or Judah seemed to appreciate.

After giving Mr. Marsh a few last-minute instructions about where to go in Poza Rica, Mr. Cirone handed a set of van keys and Judah's pouch of legal documents to him, embraced him quickly, and sent him to catch up.

I moved a bit closer to Rebekah. "He'll be okay."

"I know."

"Does it make it any easier—not being able to go with him— now that he's doing so much better?"

"A little." Then, without turning to face me, she said, "He told me what you said last night."

That surprised me. *When?*

"I mean, we just had a second, and we weren't exactly alone, so he couldn't say too much. But he said enough." Now she looked at me, and she was smiling. "It means a lot to me . . . for him."

I didn't know how to respond, so I stayed quiet.

OUT OF HIDING

Out in the plaza, several small children approached Judah. The men carrying him slowed down. One of the children dug into his shirt pocket, pulled something out, and placed it in Judah's hand.

"What are they doing?" Mrs. Cirone asked.

Mr. Cirone was not content to wait to find out. He hurried toward the plaza and the group of children—and now some men and women as well—gathering around Judah.

"Crosses," Shane whispered as he stepped in behind Rebekah and me. "They're giving him crosses." He tugged on my sleeve. "Like the one the little boy gave you."

I watched a girl lift a string over her head, clutch it for a moment in both hands, and then hold it out for Judah to take. From the string hung a tiny cross made of sticks tied together with red yarn, just as Shane had said. The tender way she handled it, and the seriousness with which she parted with it, showed clearly that she was giving Judah something she treasured.

Rebekah raised her hand to her mouth. Silent tears wet her cheeks.

Mr. Cirone did not step out onto the plaza.

The men carrying Judah waited until everyone who intended to do so had given him his or her cross, and then, with Mr. Marsh and the other man following them, left the village.

"Wow," Shane whispered.

Wow.

I expected the people in the plaza to hurry back into the jungle, away from us, but they didn't. While the women and children stayed at the center of the plaza along with most of the men, one person, an old man, approached Mr. Cirone. The two of them spoke for several minutes, shook hands, and then the old man returned to the plaza while Mr. Cirone walked toward us.

"What did he say?" we all wanted to know.

He did not answer until we'd followed him inside Mr. Meyer's house and Shane had shut the door. "He said that they've been afraid to talk to us because they know something terrible has happened to Dane. They didn't want to put him or themselves or us in any more danger. But, when they found out about Judah, they realized that it's not necessarily any safer to hide from their enemies than it is to face them."

"What happened to Judah had nothing to do with their enemies," I whispered.

Only Rebekah heard me. She grabbed my hand and held it tightly.

"These people want to be Christians," Mr. Cirone continued. "They want this church. They're ashamed that they've made us pay the price for it alone so far. They don't want to hide or surrender to fear anymore." He paused. "They're going to help us."

Chapter 16

The breakfast we ate that morning was the best we'd had in Mexico. Not because the food was any different, but because we ate it in the plaza with the village's many believers. The language barriers hindered conversation but didn't detract from an instant sense of oneness. Finally, we knew whom we'd been laboring for, and that it hadn't been, and wasn't going to be, for nothing. And they, by opposing their fear, had freed themselves to welcome and embrace us the way they'd wanted to and planned to before Mr. Meyer's disappearance.

Immediately after the meal, we began work on the building. With several men from the village helping—men who manipulated the poles and vines with practiced proficiency—it soon became clear that we had gone from having too few hands (and slow ones, at that!) to having too many. Because of this, Mr. Cirone gave us kids frequent breaks, encouraging us to spend time with the people in the plaza.

But not everyone in the village was eager to associate with us. Rebekah and I noticed several people lingering near the trees around the perimeter of the plaza, watching us . . . some with curiosity, and others with suspicion and flat-out animosity.

"I didn't realize there were so many people in this village," Rebekah whispered to me as we walked out onto the plaza.

"Neither did I." I followed her toward a group of women sitting in front of the market where we'd been buying our tortillas and bread. "Maybe some of them came down from the villages farther in."

She nodded. "That's kind of a scary thought, though."

Considering that the local drug lord and his entourage lived "farther in" and had already proven themselves committed to keeping Christianity out of their territory, I had to nod in agreement. In an effort to keep my imagination from convincing me that every person lurking in the shadows of the plaza was an armed felon, I forced myself to look at—and think about—Rebekah.

"Are you doing okay?" I asked her. "About Judah?"

"Yeah."

"Good." *Okay. So . . . now what?*

"So, Ashton," she said, "I haven't really gotten to know you on this trip. I mean, I know *about* you, and I thought I had you pretty much figured out. But what you did last night . . . well, I was wrong. I don't know you at all. And I want to." She gently grabbed my arm and led me to a wooden bench in the shade of a huge tree—a tree with no "felons" around it, I couldn't help noticing. She sat down. "What do you like to do?"

I sat beside her. "Outdoor stuff, mostly. Hiking. Skiing. Snowmobiling. Riding horses . . . at least, I used to like that. I haven't been allowed to since . . . since Tommy." Seeing discomfort in her eyes, I hurried to add basketball to my list. "What about you?"

"You're going to think I'm boring," she said, "but I like to write." She looked nervously across the plaza. "Not very adventurous, huh?"

I shrugged. "Adventure isn't always everything it's advertised to be. How'd you get into writing?"

"This might sound stupid," she said, "but when I realized that . . . that I . . . that Judah might be . . . well, that my feelings for him were . . ."

I laughed. "Don't be shy, Rebekah. Everybody on this trip has you two married in less than five years." I leaned toward her. "You should hear Hope and Callie!"

"They do not!"

I raised my hands. "Ask them, if you don't believe me."

Her face flushed with embarrassment but quickly turned serious again. "I shouldn't be talking about Judah to you, Ashton. I know you'll never think about him without thinking of your brother, and I don't mean to—"

I looked straight at her and hoped she'd understand what I was about to confide to her. "What I want, Rebekah, *is* to think about my brother, and Judah, and everything else. I've been refusing to for so long that it's kind of like I stopped living. I can't pretend that Tommy didn't die or that it doesn't bother me that he did die, any more than these people in the village can pretend they're not afraid now that they've openly sided with us. I have to deal with what happened. I have to deal with Judah and what's inside me toward him. I've done it wrong long enough." Letting out a shaky breath, I leaned back against the tree. "So . . . when you realized you might love Judah . . . ?"

"I . . ." Rebekah leaned back against the tree too. Shoulder to shoulder with me. "I started keeping a journal. You know, about my feelings. About Scriptures I would read, or teaching I would get about the appropriate ways to relate to one another. Hints I might get from him that maybe he feels the same way."

I laughed. "I hope you're not still looking for those?"

"No." She smiled. "I know how he feels about me. Anyway, I wrote everything down, figuring it would either be something I could share with him after we got married, or something I could shred and burn if he ended up breaking my heart." She paused for a long moment. "Out of that, I realized that I liked to write and could probably be good at it if I worked a little. I decided to try some poetry. A story or two." She shrugged. "I've never shown them to anyone to know whether they're any good or not, but I know I had fun writing them."

"Do you still keep your journal?" I asked her.

"Yeah. I didn't bring it with me, though. It's at home." Quickly, she pushed herself away from the tree and leaned forward until her elbows could rest on her knees. "The last time I wrote in it, I was mad at him."

I didn't ask *why*, because I knew that *that* wasn't the thing troubling her now. I leaned forward and placed my hand on her shoulder. "Do you want me to pray with you?"

She nodded.

When I finished, I leaned against the tree again and shut my eyes. I'd told Rebekah that I needed to start thinking and talking about Tommy . . . and Judah. Well, I had. It hadn't been difficult, exactly. But it hadn't been easy either.

Old and tired defenses had been right there to gang up on me. The same reasoning. *This is going to hurt. It would be easier to think about something else. What good is it going to do to dredge up pain?*

The bondage I thought I'd ousted forever when I decided to face things and learn to live with them rather than hide from them was still loitering, ready to move back into my heart. But I was determined to find peace for the situation and my feelings about it. To do that, I'd have to let myself experience those feelings, one at a time, and figure out what God would want me to do with them.

"Ashton?"

I opened my eyes to find Rebekah sitting sideways on the bench, looking intently at me. "Yeah?"

"Do you want me to pray with you?"

"I could definitely use it," I admitted.

Her words, as she placed her hand on my arm and quietly began to pray, immediately penetrated my exact need . . . respectfully and without condemnation.

We sat without speaking for several minutes after she finished. I kept my eyes closed and savored the sounds of the plaza in front of us—conversation, laughter, hammering, chickens and pigs, and the gentle rustling of the branches above us. I had not experienced a moment as peaceful in months . . . maybe longer.

"We should get back." Rebekah stood and observed the work in progress at the church site. "Somehow, I doubt they're going to need us at the building. Maybe we can help with lunch, or something."

But even among the women of the village, Hope, Callie, Rebekah, and I felt conspicuously in the way. They treated us graciously enough, responding with gratitude to our efforts to "assist" them . . . but we all knew that they could have prepared the meal just as quickly—if not more quickly—without us. Still, helping them was fun—grinding, pounding, patting, and rolling tortillas on a three-legged black stone slab which the women called *metate*. We learned to use the *mano al metate*, a rounded stone cylinder that looked like a rolling pin except that it had no handles, narrowing instead to points on the ends. My arms ached when we finished, but I knew that I'd never reach into the refrigerator for one of those reclosable plastic bags of tortillas without remembering this experience . . . The heat of the sun on my shoulders as I'd worked. The cool, gritty texture of the earthenware mortar and pestle—*molcajete y moledor*. The fresh and incontestable flavor of the "real" thing.

During the afternoon, Rebekah, Mr. Cirone, and I worked with Moises, one of the men who'd hiked in from the village at the bottom of the trail. By three o'clock, the air hung so thick and heavy with moisture, and was so unmercifully hot, that everyone began to slow down.

Moises finished tightening vines around two more poles and then stepped away from the wall, rubbing his palms together and squinting up at the sky. "*Aguaceros*," he said.

Rebekah and I looked at Mr. Cirone, who translated, "Summer rains."

All at once, as if the sky had somehow signaled them, everyone from the villages stopped working and headed either to Mr. Meyer's house, or to their own houses.

The sun was still shining, but the sky had definitely grayed since the last time I'd looked up at it. A breeze that seemed to come from everywhere first crept and then sped through the jungle around us, pushing entire plants back and forth so that their leaves looked to be waving.

"What do you say we go inside?" Mr. Cirone had to shout over the rising wind. He grinned as if he'd thought of the idea himself.

Nobody argued.

We'd barely pulled Mr. Meyer's door shut when the rain began to fall. Huge drops pummeled the roof above our heads and vaporized when they hit the hot ground. It fell faster, larger, and harder until we could hardly speak to one another over the noise on the roof and the thunder. One of the women who'd taken refuge in Mr. Meyer's house began to move our things away from the walls, piling them on a high spot in the center of the floor.

For two hours or more, the storm seemed to do nothing but intensify the muggy heat. The rain itself was warm. Not just lukewarm. *Warm.* But eventually, as afternoon turned to evening, the drops became smaller and began to fall less steadily, and the breeze whistling through every crack in the wall grew cooler.

"Maybe I'm not going to die," Hope muttered. She stepped in front of one of the windows to relish it.

Too soon, just as the storm began to be pleasant, it dissipated. The sun shone down in warm misty rays on all the wet green, and the air smelled like the bamboo walls of the church building. We walked as a group to the plaza to buy dinner from the old man's market, but some of the women had brought out bread, fruit, and coffee, so we ate that instead.

I sat alone on the same wooden bench Rebekah and I had used earlier.

Rebekah and Callie joined me. "I can't believe how much coffee people drink here," Rebekah said.

I nodded. I didn't mind. I liked coffee. Then I turned to look straight at Callie. "I'm really sorry about your mom," I said. "My brother died two years ago. Maybe we can go for a walk or something later and talk." I smiled. "Maybe it would help. Maybe we could help each other."

Callie nodded. "Thanks, Ashton," she said quietly. "I'd like that."

Shane approached us then, running. "Look!" He pointed toward the end of the plaza where the trail met up with the village.

The three men who'd gone out with Mr. Marsh and Judah that morning!

Mr. Cirone saw them too. After excusing himself from a conversation, he hurried with his wife to meet them.

The entire plaza grew quiet.

Beside me, Rebekah gripped the edge of the bench with both hands.

Confused between wanting to squeeze her hand to let her know I was there for her and feeling afraid to because *I* was the reason any of this had happened in the first place, I did not lift my hand from the bench.

At last, Mr. and Mrs. Cirone turned toward us again. They were smiling.

Mrs. Cirone returned to the center of the plaza with the three men to share the apparently good news with everyone there. Mr. Cirone approached Shane, Rebekah, Callie, and me. He looked steadily at each of us. First Shane. Then me and Callie. Then Rebekah. "Sounds like he's going to be fine," he said. "They said he absolutely refused to be carried any farther than about half a mile down and walked the rest of the way himself without any problems."

Shane grinned. "I knew it! I mean, he'd have had to be comatose to lie there and let those poor guys carry him the whole way down that trail."

"I have to admit, Shane," Mr. Cirone said, "that as much as I think it would have been better for him to let them, the fact that he felt well enough to refuse to makes me really happy right now." He paused. "Anyway, they sent Ernesto—he's the pastor of

Moises's church—with Mr. Marsh because he knows an excellent doctor in Poza Rica and exactly where to find him. I figure they'll be back by the day after tomorrow."

"Even Judah?" Shane asked.

"If the doctor sees no reason to send him home, and if his parents give their permission for him to stay. Otherwise, Mr. Marsh will get him to an airport and put him on a plane home." He shrugged. "His cut still looked pretty clean this morning. His fever's down. My guess is he'll be staying."

Chapter 17

That night, I did not dream. I slept so well and so soundly, in fact, that Mrs. Cirone had to shake me awake to keep me from sleeping straight through breakfast.

I ate quickly and then walked with Mrs. Cirone and the rest of the girls down to the river. One at a time, while the others stood on the bank and kept watch, we bathed. Though I would still prefer a cool shower in the privacy and cleanliness of an indoor bathroom, I'd begun to appreciate these river baths. The water felt relatively cool compared to the morning air, and the gentle current pushing against and around me when I leaned my head back to rinse my hair relaxed and refreshed me. For a few brief moments, I could savor the feeling of being *clean*. No sticky sunscreen on my skin. No dirt. No insect repellent. No sweat.

But only for a few minutes. Then we went back to work.

Rebekah and I worked with two teenage boys from the village, Cirilo and Pascasio, weaving vines through the edges of the roof structure and around the tops of the bamboo poles to secure it more tightly to the walls.

For most of the morning, Cirilo and Pascasio behaved as if working with us either unnerved or annoyed them. Whether this was because we were from the U.S., or because we were girls, or because we were girls from the U.S., Rebekah and I couldn't guess. Whatever the reason, their apparent uneasiness served only to make us uneasy too. But gradually, Cirilo and Rebekah discovered that they each knew just enough Spanish to communicate with one another. So, laboring at first over every word, and sometimes requiring several attempts at the same sentence to either understand or be understood, they began to talk.

Cirilo wanted to know about the United States. About our schools. Television. He wondered if either of us owned an airplane. He asked us how long it had taken us to drive down to Mexico and how much the trip had cost. He asked us what our church buildings looked like.

When Rebekah explained that both of our church buildings had to be made of sturdier materials because it snowed where we lived, his eyes sparkled. He told us that he'd often wondered what it would be like to wake up in a world covered in white.

He pointed toward a path through the jungle and said that we could find the teacher's house if we went that way, though a teacher would not hike in again until the start of the new school year. Both Cirilo and Pascasio had attended school only through grade six because any education beyond that had to be paid for. This seemed to bother Cirilo, but not Pascasio. As far as Pascasio was concerned, life was life and could never be any different— and he didn't want it to be, especially now that he knew Jesus.

Both boys had so many questions that, by lunch time, with Rebekah and Cirilo translating everything for Pascasio and me, the four of us had devoted so much time and close attention to our conversation that we'd only accomplished half as much work as the team beside us.

But nobody seemed to mind.

After lunch, Mr. Cirone asked Rebekah and me to help with the dishes. We went with a mother and daughter, Lourdes and Cayetana. We carried the dirty bowls and utensils in several large baskets to a huge metal tub behind the shop where Mr. Cirone had been buying our meals. The old man, who'd not come into the plaza all day, peeked out at us but said nothing.

Neither Lourdes nor Cayetana spoke as much Spanish as Cirilo, so we washed the dishes without a lot of conversation. That suited me—only because I knew that the old man was just on the other side of the stick wall. Cirilo had told us that there were

Christians in the village still too frightened to come out and meet us. Was this old man one of them? If not, was he opposed to us, or merely neutral? Since I had no way of knowing, his presence intimidated me.

I tried to focus on the dirty spoons at my fingertips in the tub of water but found my attention drawn instead to Cayetana. Her long black hair had come loose from her braid in several places. Her clothes didn't fit her exactly right. Her hands, though she was no older than Rebekah or me, looked rough and worn already. But she was beautiful. Dark eyes. A frequent and shy smile that seemed not to notice her hunched position over the tub of water or the pile of dishes still waiting to be washed. It seemed unfair that this girl would probably never know the enjoyment of having her hair put up by a professional stylist, or of standing in front of a three-way mirror to try on dresses for some special occasion, or of having her picture taken for a high school yearbook. All of these experiences would be considered matter-of-course back home. Girls expected them and hardly appreciated them. Myself included.

When all the dishes had been washed, dried, and returned to the women who owned them, I gently took Cayetana by the hand. I pointed toward Mr. Meyer's house and smiled at her. I hoped she'd understand that I wanted her to come with me.

She seemed to, and after getting a nod of permission from her mother, she walked with me past the nearly finished church building and inside the house.

I sat on my sleeping bag, waited for her to sit beside me, and then reached into my pack for my hairbrush and one of my favorite clips—a gold oval that surrounded off-white lace. I showed them to Cayetana and then reached forward and touched her hair.

Slowly, she nodded.

When she'd turned around so that I could sit behind her, I carefully undid her braid. After brushing her thick hair for several minutes, I experimented with several braids, buns, and rolls, but finally decided on a loose French twist. Because I wasn't used to doing someone else's hair—only my own, I had to redo it several times and still wasn't completely satisfied. But, when I slid the clip in, pulled my hands away, and walked on my knees around Cayetana so I could see her from the front, I smiled. "*Muy bonita,* Cayetana."

Very pretty. Actually, she looked gorgeous, but I didn't know how to say that. *Muy bonita* would have to suffice.

She stared into the mirror I'd gotten out of my pack. "*Gracias,* Ashton."

I did not correct her mispronunciation of my name. *Oshteen.*

Carefully setting the mirror facedown on my sleeping bag, she held her hand out for the brush.

Did she dislike the French twist? Had I offended her?

But Cayetana did not reach for her own hair. She reached for mine.

When Rebekah entered the house ten minutes later, looking for me, she folded her arms across her chest and pretended to pout. "Sure, Ashton. Leave me to help dump the dishwater while you go get your hair done!" She walked across the room to examine first Cayetana's hair and then mine. As she stepped away from me after admiring my hair from every side, she smiled and nodded appreciatively to Cayetana. "*Se ve muy bien.*"

It looks very good.

So Cayetana braided Rebekah's hair too.

The three of us walked outside to meet the stares of the people working beside the church building . . . a particularly fond stare from Pascasio, I noticed. Cayetana acknowledged his stare with a warm and half-embarrassed smile and then walked away from all of us toward the plaza.

"That smile needs no interpretation," Rebekah whispered to me with a smile of her own.

I decided to see if I could put a little red in her cheeks. "I guess some things are the same everywhere."

She blushed instantly.

Mr. Cirone waved to us from the front of the church building. "Come help Shane with these last few poles, will you? I'm going to help the men get started on building benches."

"Benches." Rebekah shook her head as we approached Shane and the unbelievably small pile of remaining poles. "I can't believe how much we've gotten done these last few days. When we first started, I thought we'd never finish."

"And we didn't." I watched several men as they carried flat planks of wood to a clear spot beside the building. "They did."

"That's true."

For the rest of that afternoon, as Mr. Cirone and several men from the village began to build benches and a group of teens used shovels and brooms to fill in and pack the dirt around the base of the walls, Rebekah, Shane, and I put the last poles up and used the last of the cut vines to secure them in place. Shane clipped the ends off the vines, and I looped the excess four or five times around the final support beam. Then we walked inside the building.

It had no windows, and a three-foot-wide gap in the wall would serve as the doorway. Above our heads, four loops of metal wire woven into the roof hung down around the thickest places on the support beams.

"They'll hang oil lamps from those,' Shane told me.

I nodded. Even though some light did come in through the doorway, the cracks in the walls, and the places where the poles didn't exactly meet the ceiling, the people would definitely want more.

With only a small portion of the roof left to finish adding palm leaves and grass to, and a few more benches to build, we stopped work for the day and sat together inside the building to eat the dinner the women had brought for all of us. Babies. Children. Teens. Men. Women. Americans. Mexicans.

Christians.

Well into the night we stayed there. Eating. Drinking coffee and warm soda. Talking. Listening while the children sang first Totonaco and then Spanish words to songs we knew . . . *Amazing Grace, Great Is Thy Faithfulness, Jesus Loves the Little Children* . . . and many songs we didn't know. Performing one of our skits. Praying together.

It was at the same time familiar, like church at home, and yet new.

We had no ceiling fans, no chairs, no piano, no oak pulpit, no fake plants, no sermon, no stained-glass windows—no windows *period*—and no clock on the back wall . . . and yet, we had church.

Pastor Ewen had often preached about a depth of fellowship that he believed Christ had intended for His church. A depth of fellowship, he told us, that he'd never failed to experience on the mission field, but sometimes felt robbed of in churches in the United States . . . where schedules, programs, personalities, time constraints, and our society's overall "consumer mentality" seemed to have shoved much of what is most *real* about Christian fellowship and oneness right out of the average church service. Corporate prayer. Knowing one another's burdens so you can bear them. Making doctrine as daily as life. Sharing the Lord's Supper.

During the next three days as we finished the building, tended to details (like hanging a curtain over the empty doorway), put together the rest of the benches and a pulpit, and, of course, set up an outhouse several yards into the thick jungle behind the church, I thought a lot about Pastor Ewen's remarks. While it was true that praying and laboring together and our common concern for Mr. Meyer had united our mission team with the people in this village in a real and undeniable way, it was also true that home was a very different place. Pulling off a successful Sunday morning church service in Alaska required a lot less oneness of purpose than raising a church building in the heat of the jungle in outward defiance of dangerous and antagonistic drug traffickers.

Didn't it?

That would depend on a person's definition of a "successful" church service, I supposed . . . and maybe *that* had been Pastor Ewen's whole point.

That's what I'd always most loved—and hated—about Pastor Ewen's preaching . . . the way it never allowed itself to just be heard and digested . . . and then forgotten. Even now, nearly two years after his last sermon at our church, his thoughts were making me think.

Unfortunately, I wasn't the only person with time to think or something to think about.

Several days had now passed since Mr. Marsh and Judah had left the village. They had not returned, and we'd received no word about them from any of the people from Moises's village who'd hiked up to see and rejoice in the new church here. Mr. Cirone tried to hide his concern, but I could sense it every time someone asked him about it, and in the way he'd stop working to watch the jungle and the trail coming into the village.

Even if it had turned out that Judah *did* need to be sent home early, Mr. Marsh should have been able to bring him to Poza Rica, arrange his flights, see him off, and get back here by now.

"Maybe the doctor wanted to watch him for a couple of days before deciding," I suggested to Rebekah as we washed yet another batch of dinner dishes in the tub behind the old man's *tortilleria*. She'd been quiet all afternoon, watching the trail like Mr. Cirone.

She nodded.

"Or maybe they decided to wait for us at the bottom of the trail since we have to leave the day after tomorrow anyway, rather than pushing Judah's luck by making the hike back up here."

Still washing the same bowl she'd picked up five minutes ago, she nodded again. "Maybe."

Gently, I took the bowl from her hands. "You need to think about something else, Rebekah."

"Right." She dumped a basketful of silverware into the water.

"I mean it," I pressed. "You're probably imagining all kinds of horrible things and—"

"You of all people should know that horrible things do happen." She stared at me then, clearly as stunned as I was that she'd said that. "I'm sorry, Ashton."

I tapped a spoon against the palm of my hand and said nothing.

We washed the rest of the dishes, dumped the water, and walked back onto the plaza, heading for the church and another evening meeting.

Chapter 18

"May I join you?" Mrs. Cirone whispered around Mr. Meyer's front door to Callie and me.

The two of us had been sitting outside on the bench in front of the house since just after the meeting at the church had let out. We'd been talking, praying, talking some more, and praying some more.

"Sure," I said.

She sat between us. "How are you doing, Callie?"

Callie didn't answer right away. "It helps that other people know about Mom," she said. She looked at Mrs. Cirone. "I thought I'd want to keep it with just you adults knowing . . . you know, I didn't want the other kids feeling sorry for me or not knowing how to act around me." She shook her head. "But being honest about it takes a lot of pressure off. If I'm being moody, someone'll give me a hug, or something. Before, everyone just looked at me like I was rude."

I smiled. "You *were* rude."

She laughed. "I know. But you know what I mean." She paused. "And it especially helps having Ashton to talk to . . . since she's been through kind of the same thing."

Mrs. Cirone nodded. Then she turned to me. "How about you?"

"I'm doing better." I looked down at my knees. "I just wish I knew what was going on with Judah and Mr. Marsh."

"We all do," she said. Then she asked, "Are you and Chad pretty good friends?"

I shrugged. "I guess. Why?"

"Maybe you could talk to him. He's dealing with a lot right now too . . . and he won't talk to us. We've tried."

"Mrs. Cirone," I said, "all he ever wants to do, when it comes to Judah, anyway, is fume. And to be honest, I don't want to hear it anymore. I never did."

"All right." And she let it go.

We talked for a few minutes after that about other things, until Mrs. Cirone glanced at the lighted dial of her watch and stood up. "We should go inside and get some sleep," she said. "It's two in the morning!"

Since neither Callie nor I could dispute the wisdom of that, we nodded and followed her inside. I didn't want to wake anyone, so I lay down on top of my sleeping bag without brushing my hair or pulling off my boots. Though the room was quiet, and dark except for the moonlight poking in through the cracks in the walls and along the ceiling, I could not relax enough to sleep.

Mr. Meyer.

Judah and Mr. Marsh.

The Christians in this village and the opposition they'd undoubtedly continue to face from the drug traffickers.

Each and all of these concerns competed for my attention, and none of them wanted to stay in God's hands when I tried to pray and put them there. But even if I wasn't sure that I had confidence in God to exercise His control in a way that I'd understand and appreciate, I was smart enough to know that any hope for a right end to any of these situations would have to come from Him.

So I kept praying, in spite of the nagging fearfulness that it wouldn't do any good, until I fell asleep. *Lord, I want to trust You again to be sovereign. The way I did before Tommy died. Please help me to trust You to be sovereign for Mr. Meyer, for Judah and*

Mr. Marsh, for my parents, for this church and the people here . . . for me.

And then I was dreaming . . . something about a dog, a bag of hamburgers, and a pair of army-green shoelaces . . . until someone's shouting frightened me awake.

"Something's burning! Something's on fire!"

I could see flickering gold through my eyelids even before I was fully awake. The smell of smoke hung in the air above me.

"Grab your sleeping bags!"

Mr. Cirone's voice sounded forceful but small against the splintering and popping of walls crashing in on themselves.

I got to my feet and, only vaguely aware that it wasn't Mr. Meyer's house that was burning, followed several people outside.

The church!

The bamboo walls had become walls of flame.

Had one of the oil lamps fallen to the ground . . . or had someone set this fire deliberately?

The questions would have to wait.

With our sleeping bags and buckets of water hauled up one at a time from the river, we tried to smother the flames. Their head start had obviously been significant, but minute after minute until it felt like hour after hour, we battled them anyway. I slapped my sleeping bag against the flames, dragged it in the dirt as I pulled it back toward myself, ignoring the sparks it tried to throw at me and the smell of its melting synthetic filler. I swung again so many times that my arms began to ache so much that I thought I wouldn't be able to lift them one more time. But again and again, I did. Until strong hands yanked the sleeping bag away from me, replaced it with a bucket, and shouted, *"Agua!"*

Water.

I ran for the trail to the river, grateful for the chance to breathe in clean air. Several times I filled the bucket, carried it back up, dumped water on the fire, and ran back down to the river to fill it again.

Everyone worked as hard as I did. Some worked harder. Our team members. Many people from the village.

But the fire refused to surrender until there was nothing left of the church to burn. And even then, it smoldered, blackening what remained of the crumpled and incinerated bamboo.

Only then did I notice that the sun had risen.

People lingered exhausted and silent a few feet back from the still smoking heap of debris. Our faces, arms, hands, and clothes were black. All around the perimeter of where the church had stood just yesterday, eyes and postures showed defeat.

"Well," Mr. Cirone said finally, "at least we kept it from burning anything else."

Mrs. Cirone repeated what he'd said in Spanish.

Someone from the village translated the statement in Totonaco.

Several people nodded.

A woman from the village said something in Spanish.

After he translated, "And nobody was hurt," Mr. Cirone closed his eyes and whispered a prayer of thanks to God. All around our destroyed church building and in three languages, people joined him.

Tears began to streak the soot on many faces, mine included.

For several minutes, nobody seemed to know what to do next. No fire chief was going to show up to "take charge of the scene" or offer us a toll-free number to call for posttrauma support. It was just us, the jungle, and a burned-down building. But then Mr. Cirone said, "I don't know about anyone else, but I'm hungry."

Nobody believed him, and nobody was hungry, but we all got busy cleaning ourselves up and preparing breakfast.

A breakfast eaten in sharp silence.

Though it was possible that the fire had been accidentally started by an untended oil lamp, I suspected that very few people, if any, believed that. But any speculation about the involvement of the drug traffickers went unspoken. Was this because of fear? Anger? Shock? The demoralizing probability that nothing would be done about it even if arson could be proven? I didn't know. Whatever the reason, it looked as if these people had resolved themselves to being victims of their powerful neighbors and intended to do nothing to retaliate.

As much as I failed to understand this defeated reasoning, I knew that I could not judge it. Theirs was a different culture with different rules.

A different world.

A world where it seemed to be okay with God and everyone else that we had worked all year raising money to get here to build a church—only to watch it burn down two days after we finished.

After breakfast, many people left the plaza, heading into the jungle toward their homes or toward the trail. I followed Mr. Cirone and the rest of our team back to Mr. Meyer's house, hoping that he didn't have it in mind to fortify us with one of his pep talks about God's giant puzzle again.

How could this be part of God's purpose?

How could He even allow it?

For the first time since arriving in Mexico, all I wanted to do was go home.

"I think we're all agreed that this was no accident," Mr. Cirone said quietly when we'd all found a place to sit on the dirt floor. "We said at the very beginning of all this that we'd reevaluate if things got hostile."

"I'd say they're hostile, all right," Shane said.

Mr. Cirone nodded. "We can head out right now, if that's what we want to do."

After several discouraged variations on *Might as well* from nearly all of us, Chad had to ask, "What about the people in the village? Won't they think we're abandoning them?" He stared steadily at Mr. Cirone. "And won't they be right?"

"There's nothing else we can do here," Shane argued. "We have to leave tomorrow, anyway. We can't build them another church! We don't even have materials anymore."

"Do you think we're in danger?" Chad asked Mr. Cirone.

Many of us laughed in cold disbelief. What a question! *Of course we're in danger.*

But Mr. Cirone said, "I think that if those people had wanted to harm *us,* they would have by now. I think they know there'd be some pretty serious consequences if they tried."

"That didn't stop them from hurting Mr. Meyer," Rebekah pointed out.

"That's a little different."

We had to concede to that. Mr. Meyer had been a man alone here. In doing his best to make himself part of this village and represent Christ, he'd made some formidable enemies.

"So . . . what are you saying?" I asked him.

"The same thing I've said all along. One man can disappear in the jungle, and it can be explained away and covered up. Not so with thirteen of us."

"Eleven," Rebekah corrected.

"Eleven." Mr. Cirone nodded slowly as he turned to face Chad. "My first responsibility is for the safety of the people on my team. I don't *think* the people who burned our church will hurt us, but I don't know for sure that they won't. So, as much as I don't want to leave the Christians here with the feeling that we had no commitment to them, I think we have to—"

A noise outside, above, and seemingly all around us, silenced him.

"Sounds like a helicopter," Shane said as we all scrambled to our feet and ran outside.

The noise was deafening, and—because of where we were—unnerving. We had not heard the hum or roar of any kind of engine in days. And now, to suddenly be hearing helicopters?

Matt pointed toward the sky. "Hueys!"

I wouldn't have known a Huey from any other kind of helicopter, but I took his word for it as the three machines appeared over the tops of the trees where the village interrupted the jungle.

Hueys . . . *here?*

Why?

We watched them fly over the clearing above the plaza and then disappear deeper into the jungle. Most of us kept staring skyward even when we could no longer see them, still captivated by their noise.

"Why would there be helicopters here?" Callie asked. "Is that how they take the drugs out?"

"With Hueys?" Shane shook his head. "No way."

"I don't know what they're doing," Mr. Cirone admitted. Then he started walking back toward the house. "Come on. Let's go get packed up. We'll head out of here right after lunch."

Envious of the apparent ease with which Mr. Cirone had pulled his attention away from the helicopters, but annoyed by his willingness to get on with the business at hand without getting any answers first—as if a couple of birds had just flown over and not three military helicopters—I was one of the last kids to follow him. But I did follow him. What else could I do?

It took me all of four minutes to shove my things into my pack. Without my sleeping bag, which had been destroyed along with everyone else's while trying to smother the fire, my pack was significantly lighter than it had been when we'd hiked in. Hiking out would be easy.

But leaving wouldn't be.

Like Chad, I felt guilty about running away from persecution. I knew that this was the safest thing to do and that Mr. Cirone realistically had no other option. And I had to admit that the fire had frightened me, along with the fact that those people could have as easily torched Mr. Meyer's house while all of us were sleeping inside!

Still, it seemed wrong, somehow . . . us leaving so quickly.

To give myself something else to think about, I volunteered to take the canteens to the spring to fill them.

"Take someone with you," Mr. Cirone ordered, tossing me his army-green plastic canteen.

Shane stood. "I'll go with her."

"So will I." Rebekah picked up her canteen, a dented metal one, and waited for Hope and Callie to hand theirs to her before joining Shane and me at the door.

Questions tugged at my mind as the three of us walked quickly and quietly down to the spring. The people who'd set the fire—where were they now? Still in the village? Hiding in the trees somewhere, maybe right near us? Would Cayetana, Lourdes, Pascasio, Cirilo, and the others understand why we were leaving? How would we find Mr. Marsh? Would we ever find out what had happened to Mr. Meyer? Would Judah and I be able to restore anything of our friendship? Rebekah and I had just begun to build a friendship of our own—would it continue after we all returned home and settled back into our normal lives?

But one question haunted me more than any other: Had we accomplished anything here?

Yes, I had learned a lot about myself.

Yes, we teenagers, with very different personalities and lives, had managed to work together to share the gospel and to build a church. Some of us had even succeeded at communicating in a real way with the people who lived here.

But . . . had we really accomplished anything?

The village still had no church building.

We hadn't given the people any respite from the domination of the drug traffickers . . . in fact, we may have stirred up even more hostility toward them. This wasn't the way a mission trip was supposed to turn out. It was supposed to be the highlight of a kid's life. God was supposed to show Himself strong and glorious. We were supposed to succeed.

"Shane?" Rebekah said behind me.

"Yeah?"

"Do you think it's too late for any good to come out of any of this?"

Shane answered right away. "Nope."

Chapter 19

Most of the women and children joined us for lunch in the plaza. Mr. Cirone told them that we'd be leaving right after the meal, which didn't seem to surprise them at all. They expressed no resentment or confusion, only understanding in support of the decision . . . and sadness over the fact that it had to end this way.

"I wonder where all the men are," Rebekah whispered to me. She stuffed meat into a second taco shell.

I too prepared a second taco. Not because I was hungry. I wasn't. But I knew I'd need the nourishment for the hike out. Seven miles was seven miles, even downhill. "I don't know where they went," I said.

"Do you think they could have gone to confront the drug guys about burning the church?"

Remembering the bruises on Mr. Meyer's face and having no doubt that the drug traffickers had weapons more convincing than their fists, I frowned. "I hope not, Rebekah."

She nodded and then forced herself to bite into the taco she'd made.

Few things sicken me more than eating when I'm not hungry. My throat and stomach tightened, revolting as if I'd shoved someone's dirty socks into my mouth instead of a bite of Lourde's delicious tortilla. I ate anyway. The whole taco.

When I finished, I stood and walked slowly toward Mr. Meyer's house to get ready for the hike down. Because I still had room at the top of my pack after loading all my gear into it, I'd volunteered to take some of Mr. Marsh's or Judah's things since they weren't here yet and their packs were frameless now anyway. Mr. Cirone had given me Mr. Marsh's flashlight, a couple of his sweatshirts, and Judah's first-aid packet, which I still had to pack. These items, plus a second canteen, would probably make up for the lost weight of my sleeping bag, but I couldn't complain. Mr. Cirone's pack was going to be heavier than it had been when we'd hiked in. So would Shane's. And Chad's.

A gentle tug at my elbow when I reached forward to pull open Mr. Meyer's door startled me.

Cayetana stared up at me for a moment, smiled, and then held my hair clip out to me. The one I had used to secure her hair the day I'd put it up.

I glanced at the clip, then at Cayetana, and shook my head. "You keep it," I said.

Her expression turned curious. She didn't understand.

Slowly, I folded her fingers over the clip and pushed her hand down to her side. "You keep it," I said again. "*Es Cayetana's ahora.*" I had no doubt that I had once again mangled the Spanish language, but I could tell that this time Cayetana understood. The corners of her mouth curved up in a shy smile as she reached for the end of her braid, wrapped it in a loose bun at the back of her head, and used the clip to hold it in place.

"*Muy bonita,*" I said, thinking that I'd have to try to do my hair that way sometime.

Cayetana stepped forward and quickly hugged me before running back toward the plaza. I watched her find Lourdes in front of the old man's *tortilleria*, turn around to show her the clip, and then disappear into the jungle.

Smiling, I pulled open Mr. Meyer's door and stepped inside.

Within half an hour, everyone else had returned to the house and gathered his gear, and after a short prayer led by Mr. Cirone, we walked slowly out onto the plaza for the last time.

As much as I looked forward to taking a shower again, grabbing a cold soda from a refrigerator again, and plopping down in an overstuffed easy chair on the deck while a washing machine did my laundry for me, I felt strangely sad about leaving this place. I knew I'd never forget the Christians here, or the old man's tortillas, or bathing in the river, or the foreign unintrusiveness of everyday life here. No televisions. No telephones. No noisy little league games at the park down the road. No alarm clocks. I certainly wouldn't miss the heat, though, or the bugs, or the rarely seen but always-sensed presence of the drug traffickers.

I kept my eyes on the dirt at my feet as we walked past the flattened and smoldering scraps of our church.

"Look!"

At Shane's voice, I raised my head. Along the trail Cayetana had taken out of the village, men were returning, hauling bundles of vines and bamboo poles on their shoulders. Two at a time, they entered the plaza, crossed it, and lowered their loads to the ground a few feet away from the blackened church.

"What are they doing?" Hope asked.

Mr. Cirone smiled. "My guess is they plan to rebuild."

Why? Wouldn't the drug traffickers burn down their new building too?

Two men approached Mr. Cirone, embraced him, and then spoke to him until all the others—with Cayetana right alongside Pascasio, I noticed—arrived. As a group, with the women and children too, they thanked us, said good-bye to us—*Adios*—and followed us to the edge of the plaza and the start of the trail out.

There they stopped, and we kept going.

When we'd walked little more than a quarter of a mile, Mr. Cirone halted so abruptly that Mrs. Cirone walked into him, I walked into her, and Rebekah walked into me . . . but because of the height of the packs in front of me, I couldn't see why we were stopping.

Quickly enough, though, I heard.

"You weren't supposed to head out until tomorrow, I thought."

Mr. Marsh!

I stepped forward to stand beside Mrs. Cirone.

Coming up the trail behind Mr. Marsh was Judah . . . and I could just make out a red baseball cap in the trees behind him.

Mr. Meyer!

I moved back onto the trail, grabbed Rebekah by the arm, and gently shoved her ahead of me. She quickly moved forward and positioned herself right up beside Mr. Cirone so that she could greet Judah when he joined Mr. Marsh.

After a few minutes of surprised greeting and questions answered with more questions, we turned around and marched back toward the village.

"You talk first," Mr. Cirone said to Mr. Marsh and Mr. Meyer as we walked. "How did you three end up together?"

Mr. Marsh explained. "When we got down to the bottom of the trail with Judah, Maurilio suggested that Ernesto, the pastor there, might go with us to help us find our way around Poza Rica. It turns out Dane had gotten to Ernesto's house two nights earlier, but hadn't been able to leave because people had shown up shortly after him and were watching the place around the clock. He didn't think they had seen him and didn't want them to. We got a doctor from the village, a Christian, to come by and check on Judah. He said we probably wouldn't even need to take him to Poza Rica. He looked fine. But after dark, hoping that anyone watching wouldn't be able to see who was who in the confusion, we made a little scene about deciding to take him anyway and sneaked Dane into the van with us. We must have fooled them because nobody followed us."

"I contacted local authorities once we got to Poza Rica," Mr. Meyer added, "as well as the U.S. consulate. It took a couple days to connect with the right people, but we finally did. They said they'd get someone up there this morning to check it out."

"This morning?" Mr. Cirone asked.

"Yeah." Mr. Meyer stayed silent a moment. "Didn't they come through the village?"

"I didn't see—"

"The Hueys!" Shane remembered. "We saw three Hueys flying over this morning. Would they go up there in Hueys?"

"Could be," Mr. Meyer answered. "Those people did abduct a U.S. citizen, on top of everything else illegal they're doing."

"Wow," Shane whispered. He was obviously a big fan of anything military and considered it "cool" to be part of an international drug "incident."

Boys!

"So now it's your turn," Mr. Marsh said. "Why did you come out a day earlier than you'd planned?"

Silence.

Finally, Mr. Cirone answered, "You're not going to like what I'm going to tell you."

More silence.

"The . . uh . . . the church burned down." Mr. Cirone paused. "We figured it could have been deliberate, so we thought it wisest to leave."

"Good thinking," Mr. Meyer agreed.

Nobody said anything else until we arrived back at the village.

Several people had remained in the plaza to begin packing down and burying the charred remains of our building. Their expressions changed from exhausted to concerned when they looked up from their work and saw us. But as soon as Mr. Meyer stepped out onto the plaza, every shovel dropped to the dirt as men, women, and children ran to meet him with tearful smiles, pats on the back, and many joyful and relieved embraces. "*Gatlan,*" he said, again and again, greeting each person individually.

I watched them for a couple of minutes before turning away to pull off my pack. Somehow, I doubted that we'd be leaving again within the next few minutes.

"Ash?"

Judah. I leaned my pack against a tree trunk and then stood up straight to face him. "You look a lot better than the last time I saw you," I said.

He nodded.

"I'm glad you're okay." I kept looking directly at him. No hateful feelings. "I mean it."

He shoved his hands in his pockets, glanced at a nearby tree, and then slowly and uncertainly looked back up at me.

Most people might wonder why he was behaving so reluctantly, but I didn't. We had grown up together. I knew him. He wanted to ask me a question, but was still deciding either how to word it or if he should even ask it at all. I smiled. "Yes, Judah, I really did apologize. You weren't delirious."

He said nothing.

Had I misread him? I didn't think so. I'd guessed at his question and had probably gotten it wrong . . . or hadn't yet answered all of it.

As I took a step toward him, I remembered the Scripture Mrs. Cirone had quoted to me from Isaiah about the bruised reed. I could see one in my mind. A tall stalk, bent and broken halfway up, leaning toward the ground. Maybe hail had damaged it, or something had trampled it, or an enemy had attacked it at the root. In any case, it would certainly have died if someone hadn't come along, stood it back up, and provided it with something to lean against until that bruised place healed enough for the roots to get nourishment through it again.

"A bruised reed shall he not break, and the smoking flax shall he not quench: he shall bring forth judgment unto truth."

Well, Someone had come along and helped me up, and it felt good to be standing again. I would not turn back, no matter how much of a battle it would prove to be at times. But Judah didn't need to know all that. He needed to know only one thing. I said, "I haven't changed my mind." I stopped walking right in front of him. "And I won't."

"So what happens now," he asked nervously, "between us?"

"That, I don't know."

"Time will tell, I guess," he said.

I nodded.

When I turned away from him a few seconds later since there didn't seem to be anything else to say, I noticed Chad standing nearby, watching us. I didn't know how long he had been there, . . . and I realized that it really didn't matter. Judah and I were moving in the right direction. If Chad Reese had a problem with that . . . too bad.

Slowly, Chad stepped away from the building he'd been leaning against and walked toward us.

Judah pulled in and then let out a long, tense breath. He and Chad had not spoken face to face on this trip. The closest they'd come had been the conversation they'd had with the Cirones and Mr. Marsh, which had undoubtedly been as bare of emotion as possible.

I stood beside Judah, wishing that I'd done as Mrs. Cirone had suggested and talked to Chad. But I hadn't . . . and now I had no idea what to expect from him.

He stopped walking right in front of Judah. "I still think you should have gone with Tommy," he said quietly.

Just as quietly, Judah replied, "So do I, sometimes."

They stood there for a few seconds until first Chad, and then Judah, walked away toward the plaza.

Eventually, having little idea what I had just witnessed except that it seemed to have satisfied both boys, I followed.

Chapter 20

Mr. Meyer had to feel like nothing less than a hero.

Throughout the afternoon, people from his village plus those from the villages farther up the trail surrounded him, clung to him, and tended to his every need—from serving him a meal to bringing him a poultice for the still healing reminders on his face of the beating he'd taken from the drug traffickers.

Leaving Mr. Meyer to visit with his people, Mr. Cirone gathered our team together and assigned us jobs at the church site. While Todd, Matt, Alec, Hope, and Callie hauled water up to douse the ashes that were still smoldering, Chad, Shane, Judah, Rebekah, and I began removing shovelfuls of debris.

"I still can't believe they burned down the building," Judah commented as he used a shovel to fill in and then level the ground where Shane had just finished hauling away wet ashes.

"I know it," Shane said.

"*They* might not have done it," I pointed out because someone needed to say so.

Everyone nodded politely.

Somehow "innocent until proven guilty" didn't seem doable in this situation. We knew from Mr. Meyer's journal that buildings had been burned down in the past in retaliation to the gospel. And we needed only look at the plaza, at Mr. Meyer's face, to know that the opposition and hostility that had inspired those burnings still remained.

Would they back off now that Mr. Meyer had exposed them to people who appeared to be willing to do something about their crimes?

I hoped so.

I wondered what kind of punishment a drug trafficker who'd attempted to make a U.S. citizen vanish without explanation could expect to receive here in Mexico. I opened my mouth to pose the question to the other kids, but shut it again when I heard the hum of engines in the distance. The noise grew louder and louder as it came nearer and nearer the village until, finally, we could see the helicopters. All three of them. Flying over the plaza.

Now what are they doing? I wondered. They'd obviously picked up no passengers. Had they flown all that way just to tell the drug guys to be nicer to their neighbors from now on? Maybe they hadn't even come here because of the drug traffickers. Maybe they'd been sent on a totally unrelated mission.

But . . . what other mission could there be in the middle of this jungle?

My shoulders tensed with each answerless question until I began to recognize fear's squeeze in my stomach and its dryness in my mouth. And questions kept coming until a shrill whistle blown in the plaza silenced my mind and brought me instantly to my feet. I followed the other kids in almost a run toward Mr. and Mrs. Cirone, who had joined Mr. Meyer in front of the old man's *tortilleria.*

"What's going on?" several of us whispered.

Nobody knew.

Even the people who lived here could only stare into the jungle, waiting, just like us.

Fortunately, we didn't have to wait long.

Two men dressed in military gear—machine guns included—entered the plaza on the trail that came down from the villages further in. Behind them, a third armed man stepped back to let several people pass by him. People whose hands had been secured behind their backs. Three more armed men followed them out.

As the people passed by us, right through the center of the plaza, I realized that I had seen many of them in the village at the bottom of the trail. A couple of the older men who had stayed in the shadows to watch our skits. One of the vendors. The three teenagers who had attacked me. The old man with the scar on his face who had scared them away.

The plaza went completely silent.

The people who lived here knew who these men were.

Fear tried to settle around and through us like the first touches of a too early winter. Cold. Indisputable. Unwelcome. But like many early snowfalls, it failed to stick . . . because it was beginning to look very much as if the people of this village would never again have to fear these men. No one lowered his eyes or looked away as the drug traffickers were forced to walk right by us. And it did seem as though the soldiers were keeping the pace deliberately slow.

Was this public humiliation a designed part of their punishment or simply a consequence of trying to remove the men from the area in the most expedient way—by using the trail and therefore passing straight through the villages? I didn't know. I did know that I didn't find myself feeling particularly sorry for them.

The old man stared hatefully at me as he was led past me. Clearly, he recognized me. And maybe he was regretting the fact that he'd scared those three boys away. After all, if Judah, Shane, or I had been hurt that day, our team probably wouldn't have hiked up to the village . . . at least, not when we had. I wouldn't have run into Mr. Meyer in the jungle. Judah wouldn't have had to be carried out of here. And . . . Mr. Meyer may not have gotten an opportunity to get out of Ernesto's house for help.

But the old man couldn't know all that.

Could he?

I supposed it didn't matter. *I* knew it. It was just as Mr. Cirone had said. All these pieces had fallen into place. Like a puzzle.

God's puzzle.

I stared right back at the old man and did not look down until he'd gone by.

One of the uniformed men stopped briefly to speak with Mr. Meyer. The drug traffickers kept moving through the plaza until they reached the trail at the other end and then disappeared into the jungle for the rest of the walk down the mountain.

After several silent moments, people began to disperse and get back to whatever it was they had been doing when the drug traffickers had been led into the plaza. Conversation was quick and excited. Everyone was stunned. Pleased. Awed.

Including me. Though I still failed to see how my brother's death could fit into any puzzle with God's name on it, I had to admit that He had pieced some very frightening situations together during this trip, with several indisputable end results. Perhaps someday He'd allow me a glimpse at how the pieces of my life all fit together. Maybe then I'd understand what part Tommy's drowning had played in the overall picture. Maybe then it would make sense.

But for now, I knew that God *could* make it make sense, and that made me feel as if half of the battle was already out of the way. The more difficult half. We spent most of that last night in the village in the open plaza, celebrating freedom. The authorities had assured the leaders of the villages and Mr. Meyer that the entire drug "crop" at the end of the trail would be confiscated, that all the buildings there would be burned, and that the people themselves, particularly those who had been in charge of the operation, would be kept very far away for a very long time. Everyone was hopeful that they could keep other drug traffickers out of the area entirely, or at least from establishing any sort of power over the people in the villages.

They would rebuild the church.

We slept on Mr. Meyer's floor on blankets the women had brought for us and said good-bye for real early the next morning. With Judah carrying Rebekah's pack and Mr. Marsh carrying Hope's—so she wouldn't die—we made our way down the trail, climbed into our vans, and drove north . . . for home.

Chapter 21

I folded Shane's letter, placed it on top of my stationery box, and shut my desk drawer. Since arriving home three weeks ago from Mexico, I'd received eight letters. Two from Judah. One each from Rebekah, Callie, and Mrs. Cirone. And three from Shane.

It impressed me that you never screamed at bugs, Shane had written in the letter I'd just finished reading. *I still can't believe how you helped me on that bridge. You're the only girl I know who wouldn't have been too afraid to do that, especially with Mr. Cirone standing right there to do it instead if you hadn't offered. I bet you're not afraid to face anything.*

Shane had no idea how truly terrified I had been that day at the bridge! And I wasn't planning to clue him in. If he knew, he might not think so highly of me now. *Or would he?* And I'd never talked to him about Tommy's death or the two years I'd spent afterwards ignoring any and all feelings about it. Maybe I'd write to him about it all . . . someday.

And, as far as not being afraid to face anything . . .

I pulled my curtain back and looked out my window toward the lake. Sure enough, Dad was standing out on the dock.

I let go of my curtain, stood, and walked slowly downstairs and outside. I hadn't yet told my parents that Judah had been in Mexico. I'd made sure that I'd been the one to walk to the end of the road each afternoon to get the mail, so I knew that they hadn't seen any of the letters that had come for me. I wasn't worried so much about talking to my mother about Judah and about what had happened inside me toward him during the trip. I'd always suspected that she'd never blamed Judah for Tommy's death . . . though she'd never said that. The Ewens simply were not mentioned in our house. Ever.

Because my father *had* blamed Judah.

I had no idea how he felt about it now. We'd never talked about it. So I had no reason to think he'd changed his opinion. And that's why I'd put off talking to him about Mexico.

I bet you're not afraid to face anything.

Yes. I was afraid. But it was time.

"Hey, Dad." I stepped onto the dock. It was moving a bit more than it usually did because of the wind on the water. Waves. Big ones. The wood was wet.

"Hey, Sweetie." Dad put his arm around me when I stepped in next to him at the rail.

I decided that the best thing to do was tell him everything. All at once. Start at the beginning and not stop until *And then it was time to come home.*

And that's exactly what I did.

After a pause, Dad said quietly, "Didn't I tell you God could do amazing things on a mission trip?"

"Yeah . . ." That was not what I had expected.

Dad lowered his arm, put his hands on my shoulders, and turned me to face him. "I owe you an apology."

"You . . . what?"

"I . . . uh . . ." He had to clear his throat to get his voice out. "It's just that I'm supposed to be the leader of this family, and, well . . . I guess I knew right from the beginning that God wanted forgiveness. I mean, that's who He is. At first, though, I didn't let myself hear Him." He shook his head. "I didn't want to hear Him; I wanted to stay angry. That's what it came down to. It was easier that way."

"I understand," I told him. "I wanted to pretend everything was okay. I wanted to pretend that I'd handled it."

He nodded, pulled his hands from my shoulders, and turned back to the rail. "The Lord has been speaking to me lately—that I've been wrong. Not only about choosing to stay angry but about blaming Judah at all. About not forgiving him—if he even needs to be forgiven. Tommy was in the wrong."

He looked down at the water. "It seems, after everything, that I need to be forgiven as much as anyone."

I could hear in my father's voice that it was a struggle for him to say these words. Especially aloud. But he'd clearly come to believe them. Just as I had.

A moose stepped out of the trees on the shore of the lake directly opposite us. He put his head down to eat, looked back up at the water and at us, then disappeared into the forest again.

"I have an idea!" Dad said suddenly. When he turned to face me, he was smiling.

"What?" He'd startled me. "What's your idea?"

"You know how your mother keeps talking about going somewhere for Christmas vacation this year?"

I nodded.

"What if we go to Colorado?"

"Colorado, Dad?"

"Yeah. We can go skiing, and snowmobiling, and . . ."

"And we could see the Ewens."

"And we could see the Ewens," Dad repeated. "Unless they don't want to see us."

"I think they will, Dad," I said.

"Okay, then. We'll go inside in a while and see what your mom thinks."

I leaned in close to my father at the rail, and we looked out over the water together. It was huge, and gray, and choppy, just like the sky. For the first time, I didn't hide from the memories of my brother that always came during silence on the dock.

I allowed myself to welcome them.

And I enjoyed them.